Charles Steigerwalt

The numismatic and war envelope collections of the late Hon.

William H. Starr

Charles Steigerwalt

The numismatic and war envelope collections of the late Hon. William H. Starr

ISBN/EAN: 9783741192739

Manufactured in Europe, USA, Canada, Australia, Japa

Cover: Foto ©Andreas Hilbeck / pixelio.de

Manufactured and distributed by brebook publishing software
(www.brebook.com)

Charles Steigerwalt

The numismatic and war envelope collections of the late Hon.

William H. Starr

THE
NUMISMATIC

AND

WAR ENVELOPE COLLECTIONS

OF THE LATE

HON. WILLIAM H. STARR,

OF

NEW LONDON, CONN.,

INCLUDING

Dollars of 1794, 1854 and 1855, half dollars of 1794, 1796, 1797, 1801, 1802, 1815, 1836 reeded, AND MANY OTHER RARE U. S. AND FOREIGN COINS.

TO BE SOLD WITHOUT RESERVE

AT THE

CENTRAL AUCTION ROOMS, LANCASTER, PA.,

FRIDAY AND SATURDAY, DECEMBER 19th and 20th, 1884.

COMMENCING AT 2 P. M.

— ———

CATALOGUED BY

CHAS. STEIGERWALT, 130 E. KING ST., LANCASTER, PA.,

WHO WILL EXECUTE ALL BIDS FREE OF COMMISSION.

THE following collection contains, among other rarities, 1794, 1854 and 1855 dollars, 1796, 1797, 1801, 1802, 1815, and other rare half dollars, specimens of all the rare dimes and half dimes except the half dime of 1802, and many other rare U. S. coins, together with a notable gathering of the Copperhead Currency of 1861–1864.

The Foreign Coins are also varied and numerous, and the miscellaneous collections have a large number of desirable pieces, both for amateurs and advanced collectors.

CATALOGUE.

Foreign Coppers.

There are but few duplicates in the following lots, and the collection is exceedingly rich in rare coins. This is especially true of the German and early Spanish coins.

1. Portugal and Brazil. Large size. Good to fine. 10 pcs.
2. Portugal and Brazil. Medium size. Good to fine. 10 pcs.
3. Portugal and Brazil. Mixed size. Good to fine. 7 pcs.
4. Greek. Mixed sixe. Good to fine. 10 pcs.
5. Turkish. Mixed sixe. Good to fine. 9 pcs.
6. Tornesi of Sicily. Mixed size. Rare. Good to fine. 10 pcs.
7. Italy. Papal. Mixed size. Fair to fine. 10 pcs.
8. Italy. Different States. Mixed size. Good to fine. 10 pcs.
9. Italy. Different States Mixed size. Good to fine. 15 pcs.
10. Russia. Large size. Good to fine. 4 pcs.
11. Russia. Medium size. Good to fine. 7 pcs.
12. Russia. Small size. Good to fine. 6 pcs.
13. Denmark. Large size. Good to fine. 6 pcs.
14. Denmark. Medium size. Good to fine. Uncirculated. 10 pcs.
15. Denmark. Small size. Good to fine. 12 pcs.
16. Sweden and Norway. Portraits. Mixed size. Good to fine. 10 pcs.
17. Sweden and Norway. Different devices. Mixed size. Good to fine. 8 pcs.
18. Sweden and Norway. Crossed arrows. Mixed size. Good to fine. 9 pcs.
19. Holland and Belgium. Mixed size. Good to fine. 12 pcs.
20. Spain. Early, rude and curious. Mixed size. Fair to fine. 10 pcs.
21. Spain. Early, rude and curious. Mixed size. Fair to fine. 10 pcs.
22. Spain. Early, rude and curious. Mixed size. Fair to fine. 10 pcs.
23. Spain. Modern coins. Medium size. Good to fine. 10 pcs.
24. Spain. Modern coins. Mixed size. Fair to fine. 9 pcs.
25. Nickel coins of South America. Good to fine. 8 pcs.
26. Uruguay. A rare lot. Good. 5 pcs.
27. Chili. 1835. Good and fine. 3 pcs.
28. Chili. 1851 and 1853. Good. 4 pcs.
29. Dominica. 1844, 1848, and 1877. Fine and uncirculated. 3 pcs.
30. Hayti. Mixed size. Good. 7 pcs.
31. Mexico and Buenos Ayres. Good. 7 pcs.
32. Venezuela. Cent and half cent. Good. 2 pcs.
33. Japan. Copper and brass. Fine and uncirculated. 10 pcs.
34. Germany. Mixed size. Fair to fine. 25 pcs.
35. Germany. Mixed size. Fair to fine. 25 pcs.
36. Germany. Mixed size. Fair to fine. 25 pcs.
37. Germany. Mixed size. Fair to fine. 25 pcs.
38. Germany. Mixed size. Fair to fine. 25 pcs.
39. Germany. Mixed size. Fair to fine. 25 pcs.
40. Germany. Mixed size. Fair to fine. 45 pcs.
41. France. From Henry III. to Louis XIV. Fair to fine. 10 pcs.
42. France. From Henry III to Louis XIV. Fair to fine. 13 pcs.
43. France. Louis XVI. Fair to fine. 8 pcs.

44. France. The First Republic. Fair to fine. 10 pcs.
45. France. Monneron Tokens. Fine and uncirculated. 2 pcs.
46. France. Napoleon I, as King of Italy. Good. 3 pcs.
47. France. Colonials. Good. 5 pcs.
48. France. Charles X. and Louis Phillipe. Good. 7 pcs.
49. France. Louis Napoleon. Good to fine. 15 pcs.
50. France. Jetons, medals and coin weights. Curious lot. Good to fine. 5 pcs.
51. England. Charles II., James II., William and Mary, George I. Fair to good. 8 pcs.
52. England. Wood halfpence. Varieties. Good. 3 pcs.
53. England. George II. Halfpence and farthings. Fair to fine. 11 pcs.
54. England. George III. Penny to farthing size. Fair to fine. 24 pcs.
55. England. George IV. Penny to farthing size. Fair to fine. 5 pcs.
56. England. Victoria. Penny to farthing size. Fair to fine. 11 pcs.
57. England. Tokens and patterns. Curious lot. Fair to fine. 12 pcs.
58. England. Guernsey and Bermuda. Fair to fine. 3 pcs.
59. England. Demarara. Good to fine. 5 pcs.
60. England. Canada. Bank tokens. Good to fine. 11 pcs.
61. England. Canada. Mixed tokens. Good to fine. 13 pcs.
62. England. Canada. Un sou tokens. Good to fine. 7 pcs.
63. England. Nova Scotia. Penny to halfpenny size. Good to fine. 15 pcs.
64. England. New Brunswick, New Foundland, Prince Edwards Island. Good to fine. 10 pcs.
65. England. Hong Kong and St. Helena. Good to fine. 6 pcs.
66. England. India. Good to fine. 15 pcs.
67. England. India. Good to fine. 10 pcs.
68. England. Tradesmen's tokens. 1794 period. Good to fine. 10 pcs.
69. England. Tradesmen's tokens. 1794 period. Good to fine. 12 pcs.
70. Siam. Pagoda. Lead. Good.
71. Roumania. 10 Bani. Good.
72. China. Cast. Small and medium size. 50 pcs.
73. China. Cast. Small and medium size. 27 pcs.
74. Belgian nickel coins, and odd bits. 19 pcs.
75. Poor and pierced coins. Many curious. 28 pcs.

U. S. Silver Dollars.

76. 1794. Stars and legend weak. Date weak, but distinct. A fair and desirable specimen of this rare coin.
77. 1795. Flowing hair. Small close date. Very fine.
78. 1795. Flowing hair. Large wide date. Good, but scratched on reverse.
79. 1795. Fillet head. Fine.
80. 1796. Large date. Good, but marred with scratches.
81. 1796. Small date. Very fine.
82. 1797. Seven stars facing. Very good.
83. 1797. Six stars facing. Good, but scratched.
84. 1798. Knobbed 9. Fine.
85. 1798. Plain 9. Fine.
86. 1799. Very good.
87. 1799. A variety. Very good.
88. 1800. Plain date. Fine.
89. 1800. Die broken at date. Fine.
90. 1801. Fine.
91. 1802 over 1801. Fine.
92. 1803. Fine.
93. 1804. Electrotype. Fine.
94. 1836. Gobrecht on base. Very fine.

95. 1838. Electrotype. Fine.
96. 1840. Fine. Mint bloom.
97. 1841. Fine. Mint bloom.
98. 1842. Very fine. Mint bloom.
99. 1843. Very fine.
100. 1845. Very fine. Mint bloom.
101. 1846. Very fine. Mint bloom.
102. 1847. Very fine. Mint bloom.
103. 1848. Very fine. Mint bloom.
104. 1849. Very fine. Mint bloom.
105. 1850. Philadelphia Mint. Very fine. Mint bloom.
106. 1850. O. Mint. Good.
107. 1853. Very fine.
107 a. 1854. Fine. Rare.
108. 1855. Very fine. Mint bloom. Reverse weakly struck. Rare.
109. 1856. Fine. Scarce.
110. 1857. Fine. Scarce.
111. 1859. Fine. Mint bloom.
112. 1859. O. Mint. Fine.
113. 1860. O. Mint. Very fine. Mint bloom.
114. 1860. O. Mint. Good. A variety.
115. 1861. Uncirculated.
116. 1862. Uncirculated.
117. 1863. Uncirculated.
118. 1864. Uncirculated.
119. 1865. Fine.
120. 1866. Uncirculated. Tarnished proof.
121. 1867. Uncirculated. Tarnished proof.
122. 1868. Uncirculated. Tarnished proof.
123. 1867. Uncirculated.
124. 1870. Uncirculated. Tarnished proof.
125. 1871. Uncirculated.
126. 1872. Fine. Mint bloom.
127. 1872. C. C. Mint. Scarce. Good.
128. 1873. Without arrows. Proof. Tarnished. Old style.
129. 1873. Trade. Uncirculated.
130. 1873. Trade. C. C. Mint. Good. Scarce.
131. 1874. Trade. Uncirculated.
132. 1875. Trade. Uncirculated.
133. 1877. Trade. Uncirculated.
134. 1877. Trade. Uncirculated. S. Mint.
135. 1878. Standard. 8 feathers in eagle's tail. Tarnished proof.
136. 1879. Trade. Brilliant proof. Scarce.
137. 1880. Trade. Brilliant proof. Scarce.

Half Dollars.

138. 1794. Fine. Strong impression. A desirable piece.
139. 1794. A variety. Fair, but everything distinct.
140. 1795. Fine. A desirable coin.
141. 1795. A variety. Good.
142. 1796. 15 stars. Obverse, all distinct. Date strong. Two nicks in the field. Reverse more rubbed, but still distinct, with a nick in the field. A good and desirable specimen of this rare date.
143. 1797. Obverse all distinct; reverse shows more wear, but still a valuable coin, and a good match to No. 142.
144. 1801. Very good for this rare date.
145. 1802. Fine for this rare date.
146. 1803. Fine and desirable. Scarce.

147. 1805. Over 4. Has been pierced and plugged, but the 4 shows very strong, and makes this a fine specimen of this overstrike.
148. 1805. Good.
149. 1805. Fine. A scarce variety.
150. 1806. Pointed 6. Very fine. Mint bloom.
151. 1806. Knobbed 6. Fine.
152. 1807. Head to right. Fine.
153. 1807. Head to left. Good.
154. 1808. Good.
155. 1809. Uncirculated. Mint bloom.
156. 1810. Fine.
157. 1811. Uncirculated. Mint bloom.
158. 1811. Uncirculated. Mint bloom. A variety.
159. 1812. Uncirculated. Mint bloom.
160. 1813. Uncirculated. Mint bloom.
161. 1814. Fine.
162. 1815. Fine, strong impression of this rare date.
163. 1817. Uncirculated.
164. 1818. Uncirculated. Mint bloom.
165. 1819. Fine.
166. 1820. Uncirculated. Beautiful.
167. 1820. Over 1819. Good and rare. Well-marked overstrike.
168. 1821. Uncirculated. Mint bloom.
169. 1822. Fine. Mint bloom.
170. 1823. Fine. Mint bloom.
171. 1824. Uncirculated. Mint bloom.
172. 1825. Uncirculated. Mint bloom.
173. 1825. Uncirculated. Mint bloom. A variety.
174. 1826. Uncirculated. Mint bloom.
175. 1827. Uncirculated. Mint bloom.
176. 1828. Large date. Curled 2. Sharp, fine, and scarce.
177. 1828. Small date. Uncirculated. Mint bloom.
178. 1829. Over 1821. Good and scarce.
179. 1829. Uncirculated. Beautiful.
180. 1830. Uncirculated. Mint bloom. Large 0.
181. 1830. Fine. Small 0. Scarce.
182. 1831. Uncirculated. Mint bloom.
183. 1832. Uncirculated. Mint bloom.
184. 1833. Uncirculated. Mint bloom.
185. 1834. Uncirculated. Mint bloom. Small date.
186. 1835. Uncirculated. Mint bloom.
187. 1836. Uncirculated. Mint bloom. Lettered edge.
188. 1836. Reeded edge. A fine impression of this rare coin.
189. 1837. Uncirculated.
190. 1838. Very fine.
191. 1839. Very fine. Head.
192. 1839. Liberty seated. No drapery below elbow. Fine. Scarce.
192a. 1839. Liberty seated. Drapery below elbow. Fine. Scarce.
193. 1840. Fine.
194. 1841. Uncirculated. Mint bloom. Scarce.
194a. 1841. O. Mint. Fine. Scarce.
195. 1842. Fine. Large date.
196. 1843. Uncirculated.
197. 1844. Very fine.
198. 1845. Very fine. O. Mint.
199. 1846. Fine. Yankee 6. Scarce.
200. 1847. Fine.
201. 1848. Fine. O. Mint.

202. 1849. Uncirculated. Mint bloom.
203. 1850. Uncirculated. Mint bloom. O. Mint.
204. 1851. Uncirculated. Mint bloom. O. Mint.
205. 1852. Uncirculated. Mint bloom. Rare.
206. 1852. Fair. O. Mint. Rare.
207. 1853. Uncirculated.
208. 1854. Uncirculated.
209. 1855. Uncirculated. O. Mint.
210. 1856. Fine.
211. 1856. Fine. O. Mint.
212. 1857. Fine.
213. 1858. Uncirculated.
214. 1859. Uncirculated.
215. 1859. Fine. O. Mint.
216. 1860. Uncirculated. Tarnished proof.
217. 1860. Fine. O. Mint.
218. 1861. Uncirculated.
219. 1862. Uncirculated. Tarnished proof.
220. 1862. Good. S. Mint. Scarce.
221. 1863. Uncirculated.
222. 1864. Uncirculated. Tarnished proof. Rare.
223. 1864. Good. S. Mint. Scarce.
224. 1865. Uncirculated. Scarce.
225. 1865. Good. S. Mint. Scarce.
226. 1866. Uncirculated. Scarce.
227. 1866. Good. S. Mint. Without "In God We Trust." Scarce.
228. 1867. Uncirculated. Tarnished proof.
229. 1868. Uncirculated.
230. 1869. Uncirculated.
231. 1870. Uncirculated.
232. 1871. Fine.
233. 1872. Uncirculated.
234. 1873. Uncirculated. Without arrows by date.
235. 1873. Uncirculated. With arrows by date.
236. 1874. Uncirculated.
237. 1875. Uncirculated.
238. 1876. Uncirculated.
239. 1877. Fine.
240. 1878. Uncirculated.
241. 1879. Uncirculated.
242. 1880. Uncirculated.
243. 1881. Uncirculated.

Quarter Dollars.

244. 1796. Good, but pierced.
245. 1804. Very fair. Rare.
246. 1805. Good. Scratched on obverse.
247. 1806. Plain date. Good. Over 1805, fair. 2 pcs.
248. 1807. Fair. Scarce.
249. 1815. Good. Scarce.
250. 1818. Very fine.
251. 1819 and 1820. Fair. 2 pcs.
252. 1820. Fine. A variety.
253. 1821. Good.
254. 1822. Fair. Scarce.
255. 1824. Good. Scarce.
256. 1825. Good.
257. 1828. Good.

DIMES.

258. 1831. Varieties. Good. 2 pcs.
259. 1832. Uncirculated.
260. 1834. Uncirculated.
261. 1835. Uncirculated.
262. 1837. Uncirculated.
263. 1838. Uncirculated. Head.
264. 1838. Fine. Liberty seated.
265. 1839. Fine.
266. 1848. Fine. Scarce.
267. 1849. Uncirculated.
268. 1850. Philadelphia and Orleans Mints. Good. 2 pcs.
269. 1851. Good. O. Mint. Scarce.
270. 1852. Very good. O. Mint. Scarce.
271. 1855. Good. S. Mint. First year of this coinage. Scarce.
272. 1858. Uncirculated.
273. 1862. Uncirculated.
274. 1863. Uncirculated. Scarce.
275. 1864. Uncirculated. Scarce.
276. 1865. Uncirculated. Scarce.
277. 1866. Uncirculated. Scarce.
278. 1867. Uncirculated. Scarce.
279. 1868. Uncirculated. Scarce.
280. 1869. Uncirculated. Scarce.
281. 1870. Uncirculated. Tarnished proof.
282. 1871. Uncirculated.
283. 1879. Uncirculated.
284. 1880. Uncirculated.
285. 1881. Uncirculated.

Dimes.

286. 1796. Very good. Scarce.
287. 1797. Good, but bent. Rare.
288. 1798 over 1797. Good. Obverse scratched. Scarce.
289. 1800. Good. Scarce.
290. 1801. Fair. Scarce.
291. 1802. Good. Scarce.
292. 1803. Good. Scarce.
293. 1804. Pierced in the centre and plugged, but a good and desirable coin of this rare date.
294. 1805. Fine.
295. 1807. Good. Bent. Scarce.
296. 1809. Fair. Scarce.
297. 1811 over 1809. Fair. Scarce.
298. 1814. Small date. Good.
299. 1814. Large date. Fine.
300. 1820. Fine.
301. 1821. Large and small dates. Fine. 2 pcs.
302. 1822. Very good for this date. Rare.
303. 1823. Very good.
304. 1824. Very good.
305. 1825. Very good.
306. 1827. Very good.
307. 1828. Large and small dates. Good. 2 pcs.
308. 1829. Uncirculated.
309. 1830. Very fine.
310. 1831. Uncirculated.
311. 1832. Uncirculated.
312. 1833. Uncirculated.

313. 1834. Uncirculated.
314. 1835. Uncirculated.
315. 1836. Very fine.
316. 1837. Very fine. Head.
317. 1837. Starless. Uncirculated.
318. 1838. Starless. Good. Scarce.
319. 1838. With stars. Fine.
320. 1839. Philadelphia Mint. Fine. O. Mint. Good. 2 pcs.
321. 1840. Drapery and no drapery. Good. 2 pcs.
322. 1841, 1842 and 1843. Fine. 3 pcs.
323. 1844. Very good. Scarce.
324. 1845. Fine.
325. 1846. Fine for date. Rare.
326. 1847, 1848, 1849, 1850 and 1851. Good and fine. 5 pcs.
327. 1852. Uncirculated. Scarce.
328. 1853. No arrows by date. Uncirculated. Scarce.
329. 1853 to 1859 inclusive. Good and fine. 9 pcs.
330. 1860. Uncirculated.
331. 1861 and 1862. Fine. 2 pcs.
332. 1863. Uncirculated. Scarce.
333. 1864. Uncirculated. Scarce.
334. 1865. Uncirculated. Scarce.
335. 1866. Uncirculated. Scarce.
336. 1867. Uncirculated. Scarce.
337. 1868. Uncirculated. Scarce.
338. 1869. Uncirculated. Scarce.
339. 1870 to 1878 inclusive. Uncirculated. 10 pcs.
340. 1879 and 1880. Uncirculated. 2 pcs.

Half Dimes.

341. 1794. Battered and partly pierced. Good and rare.
342. 1795. Very good. Scarce.
343. 1796. Fair. Bent. Scarce.
344. 1797. Fair. Bent. Rare. 13 stars.
345. 1800. Fine. Scarce.
346. 1801. Fair. Rare.
347. 1802. A fine electrotype.
348. 1803. Fair. Rare.
349. 1805. Very good. Rare.
350. 1829. Uncirculated.
351. 1830, 1831, 1832, 1833, 1834. Fine. 5 pcs.
352. 1835. Uncirculated.
353. 1835, 1836, 1837. Good. 4 pcs.
354. 1837. Starless. Uncirculated.
355. 1838. Stars. Fine.
356. 1839. P. and O. mints. Good. 2 pcs.
357. 1840. Drapery, no drapery and O. mint, fair and good. 3 pcs.
358. 1841. Good.
359. 1842. Uncirculated. Scarce.
360. 1843. Uncirculated.
361. 1844. Uncirculated. Scarce.
362. 1844. O. Mint. 1845. Good. 2 pcs.
363. 1846. Fine for date. Rare.
364. 1847. Fine.
365. 1848. Very fine.
366. 1849. Very fine.
367. 1850 and 1851. Good and fine. 2 pcs.
368. 1852. Fine. Scarce.

369. 1853. No arrows by date. Fine. Scarce
370. 1853 to 1862 inclusive. Fine to uncirculated. 10 pcs.
371. 1863. Uncirculated. Scarce.
372. 1864. Uncirculated. Scarce.
373. 1865. Uncirculated. Scarce.
374. 1866. Uncirculated. Scarce.
375. 1867. Uncirculated. Scarce.
376. 1868. Uncirculated. Scarce.
377. 1869. Uncirculated. Scarce.
378. 1870, 1871, 1872, 1873. Fine. 4 pcs.
379. 1848, 1849, 1850, 1851, 1857, 1860. O. mint. Good. 6 pcs.
380. 1863, 1866, 1868, 1872. S. mint. Good and fine. 5 pcs.

Copper Cents.

381. 1793. Stars and bars on edge. Wreath. Very fair or good.
382. 1793. Chain. Poor.
383. 1794. Varieties. Very fair. 2 pcs.
384. 1794. Fine, but nicked.
385. 1795. Thin die. Varieties. Fair and good. 2 pcs.
386. 1796. Liberty cap. Fair, nearly good.
387. 1796. Fillet head. Good. Nearly fine.
388. 1797 and 1798. Fair and good. 2 pcs.
389. 1799. A very clever alteration. Good.
390. 1800. Varieties. Good. 2 pcs.
391. 1801. Varieties. Fair. 3 pcs.
392. 1802. Stemless wreath. Very good. Scarce.
393. 1802 and 1803. Fair. 2 pcs.
394. 1803. Large $\frac{1}{100}$. Fine.
395. 1804. Genuine. Good for date. Rare.
396. 1805. Good.
397. 1806. Very good. Scarce.
398. 1807 over 1806, and plain date. Fair and good. 2 pcs.
399. 1808. Very good. Nearly fine. Scarce.
400. 1809. Good. Rare.
401. 1810. Varieties. Fair and good. 2 pcs.
402. 1811 over 1810. Good.
403. 1811. Plain date. Very good.
404. 1812. Good.
405. 1813. Good.
406. 1814. Varieties. Good. 2 pcs.
407. 1816 and 1817. Varieties. Fair and good. 3 pcs.
408. 1817. 15 stars. Very good.
409. 1818 and 1819. Varieties. Fair and good. 3 pcs.
410. 1819 over 1818. Good and rare.
411. 1820. Uncirculated. Connected stars. Scarce.
412. 1820. Overstrike and plain date. Good. 2 pcs.
413. 1821. Good.
414. 1822. Varieties. Fair and good. 2 pcs.
415. 1823. Varieties. Fair and good. 2 pcs.
416. 1824, 1825, 1826, 1827. Varieties. Good and fine. 5 pcs.
417. 1828, 1829, 1830. Varieties. Good and fine. 4 pcs.
418. 1831 to 1838 inclusive. Varieties. Good and fine. 13 pcs.
419. 1839 over 1836. Pierced. Scarce. Good.
420. 1839. Varieties. Good. 3 pcs.
421. 1840. Large date. Fine.
422. 1840 to 1845 inclusive. Good and fine. 9 pcs.
423. 1846 to 1849 inclusive. Good and fine. 7 pcs.
424. 1850 to 1856 inclusive. Good and fine. 10 pcs.

MINOR PROOF SETS.

425. 1857. Large date. Fine.
426. 1857. Small date. Fine.

Half Cents.

427. 1793. Very fair. Lettered edge.
428. 1794. Varieties. Very fair. 2 pcs.
429. 1795. Good.
430. 1796. Electrotype. Good.
431. 1797. Very fine. Scarce.
432. 1800. Very good. Scarce.
433. 1802. Very good. Rare.
434. 1803 to 1808 inclusive. Good. 6 pcs.
435. 1809. Fine.
436. 1810. Good. Scarce.
437. 1811. Fine. Rare.
438. 1825, 1826, 1828, 1829. Varieties. Good and fine. 5 pcs.
439. 1832, 1833, 1834, 1835. Good and fine. 4 pcs.
440. 1849, 1850, 1851. Good and fine. 3 pcs.
441. 1852. Electrotype.
442. 1853. Fine.
443. 1854. Fine.
444. 1855. Fine.
445. 1856. Fine. Scarce.
446. 1857. Uncirculated. Red. Scarce.

Minor Nickle and Bronze Coins.

447. 1856. Nickle cent. Flying eagle. Fine. Rare.
448. 1857 to 1864. Nickle cents. Fine to uncirculated. 8 pcs.
449. 1864 to 1882. Copper cents. Mostly bright. 17 pcs.
450. 1864 and 1865. 2 Cent Pieces. Bright and uncirculated. 2 pcs.
451. 1866 and 1867. 2 Cent Pieces. Bright and uncirculated. 2 pcs.
452. 1868 and 1869. 2 Cent Pieces. Bright and uncirculated. 2 pcs.
453. 1870. 2 cent piece. Bright and uncirculated.
454. 1871. 2 cent piece. Bright and uncirculated.
455. 1872. 2 cent piece. Bright and uncirculated.
456. 1867, 1869, 1870, 1871, 1873, 1874, 1878. 3 cent nickle. Proofs. 7 pcs.
457. 1866, 1867, 1868, 1869. 5 cent nickle. Fine and uncirculated. 4 pcs.
458. 1867, 1871, 1873. 5 cent nickle. Proofs. 3 pcs.
459. 1870, 1872, 1874, 1875, 1876, 1881 to 1883. 5 cent nickle. Uncirculated. 10 pcs.
460. 1878, 1879, 1880. 5 cent nickle. Proofs. 3 pcs.

Minor Proof Sets.

461. 1865. Slightly tarnished. Scarce. 3 pcs.
462. 1866. Slightly tarnished. Scarce. 4 pcs.
463. 1867. Slightly tarnished. Scarce. 4 pcs.
464. 1868. Slightly tarnished. Scarce. 4 pcs.
465. 1869. Slightly tarnished. Scarce. 4 pcs.
466. 1870. Slightly tarnished. Scarce. 4 pcs.
467. 1871. Slightly tarnished. Very scarce. 4 pcs.
468. 1872. Slightly tarnished. Very scarce. 4 pcs.
469. 1873. Slightly tarnished. Rare. 4 pcs.
470. 1874. Slightly tarnished. 3 pcs.
471. 1875. Slightly tarnished. 3 pcs.
472. 1876. Slightly tarnished. 3 pcs.
472a. 1877. Slightly tarnished. Very rare. 3 pcs.
473. 1878. Slightly tarnished. Scarce. 3 pcs.

474. 1879.   Slightly tarnished.   3 pcs.
475. 1880.   Slightly tarnished.   3 pcs.
476. 1881.   Slightly tarnished.   Scarce.   3 pcs.
477. 1883.   Slightly tarnished.   4 pcs.
478. 1868.   Full Proof Set.   9 pcs.

A Few Colonials, Patterns, and Copies of Scarce Coins.

479. New England three pence, six pence and shilling. Solid copies. Rare. 3 pcs.
480. 1652. Pine tree threepence. Good for this rare coin.
481. 1652. Pine tree shilling. Small planchet. Good.
482. 1792. Martha Washington half disme. Good, but pierced. Rare.
483. Connecticut cents. Rare varieties. Fair and good. 5 pcs.
484. Connecticut cents. Fair to good. Varieties. 5 pcs.
485. Connecticut cents. Fair to good. Varieties. 5 pcs.
486. Connecticut cents. Fair to good. Varieties. 3 pcs.
487. Connecticut cent. 1787. Very fine indeed.
488. Double head Washington. Good.
489. 1783. Unity and United States. Good. 2 pcs.
490. 1793. Washington halfpenny. Good.
491. 1787 and 1788. Massachusetts cents. Fair and good. 4 pcs.
492. 1787. Massachusetts half cent. Good. Rare.
493. New Jersey cents. Fair and good. Varieties. 5 pcs.
494. New Jersey cents. Fair and good. Varieties. 6 pcs.
495. 1783 and 1785. Nova Constellatio. Fair and good. Varieties. 4 pcs.
496. Vermont cents. Fair and good. Varieties. 3 pcs.
497. 1781. North American token. Good.
498. 1794. Talbot, Allum and Lee cent. Fine.
499. Nova Eborac. Fair. 2 pcs.
500. Virginia halfpence. Fair. 2 pcs.
501. Kentucky cent. Thin planchet. Fine.
502. 1787. Fugio cent. Fine.
503. 1787. Fugio cents. Fair and good. 2 pcs.
504. 1723. Wood halfpennies. Good. 2 pcs.
505. 1723. Rosa Americana twopence. Good.
506. 1722, 1723. Rosa Americana pennies. Fair. 2 pcs.
507. 1721. Louisiana cent. Very good.
508. Castorland token. Copper. Fine.
509. Washington cents. Copies. Very good and fine. 2 pcs.
510. Sommer's Island piece. Fine copper copy.
511. Granby or Higly piece. Deer and hatchets. Good copy.
512. Rosa Americana twopence. No date. Solid copper copy. Fine.
513. Immunis Columbia. Electrotype.
514. Washington cents. Fine and good. 2 pcs.
515. Copies of rare colonials in copper. 3 pcs.
516. Copies of rare colonials in lead. 6 pcs.
517. Washington half dollar 1792. Copy in white metal. Fine.
518. Gilt copy of Continental Ring Dollar. Uncirculated. A beauty.
519. Feuchtwanger cents, and model California half eagle. Good. 3 pcs.
520. Half cent's worth of pure copper. 1837. Fine. Scarce.

Store Cards and Copperheads, 1861 to 1864 Period.

In the following collection of this curious and interesting part of numismatics, the seeker after these mementos of the great war between the sections of our land, will find many valuable and rare coins. The collection comprises varieties from almost every state in which these coins were used, and gives all of the varieties of dies used. There are few if any duplicates, and the average condition of the lots makes each a good purchase:

521. Large copper size. Bright and uncirculated. 10 pcs.

522. Large copper size. Bright and uncirculated. 10 pcs.
523. Small brass size. Bright and uncirculated. 10 pcs.
524. Small brass size. Bright and uncirculated. 10 pcs.
525. Small brass size. Bright and uncirculated. 10 pcs.
526. Small brass size. Fine. 10 pcs.
527. Small copper size. Bright, brilliant red. 10 pcs.
528. Small copper size. Bright, brilliant red. 10 pcs.
529. Small copper size. Bright, brilliant red. 10 pcs.
530. Small copper size. Bright, brilliant red. 10 pcs.
531. Small copper size. Bright and uncirculated. 20 pcs.
532. Small copper size. Bright and uncirculated. 20 pcs.
533. Small copper size. Bright and uncirculated. 20 pcs.
534. Small copper size. Bright and uncirculated. 20 pcs.
535. Small copper size. Bright and uncirculated. 20 pcs.
536. Small copper size. Bright and uncirculated. 20 pcs.
537. Small copper size. Bright and uncirculated. 20 pcs.
538. Small copper size. Bright and uncirculated. 20 pcs.
545. Small copper size. Bright and uncirculated. 20 pcs.
546. Small copper size. Bright and uncirculated. 10 pcs.
547. Small copper size. Good and fine. 20 pcs.
548. Small copper size. Good and fine. 20 pcs.
549. Small copper size. Good and fine. 20 pcs.
550. Small copper size. Good and fine. 20 pcs.
551. Small copper size. Good and fine. 20 pcs.
552. Small copper size. Good and fine. 20 pcs.
553. Small copper size. Good and fine. 20 pcs.
554. Small copper size. Good and fine. 20 pcs.
555. Small copper size. Good and fine. 20 pcs.
556. Small copper size. Good and fine. 20 pcs.
557. Small copper size. Good and fine. 20 pcs.
558. Small copper size. Good and fine. 20 pcs.
559. Small copper size. Good and fine. 20 pcs.
560. Small copper size. Good and fine. 20 pcs.
561. Small copper size. Good and fine. 20 pcs.
562. Small copper size. Good and fine. 20 pcs.
563. Small copper size. Good and fine. 20 pcs.
564. Small copper size. Good and fine. 20 pcs.
565. Small copper size. Good and fine. 20 pcs.
566. Small copper size. Good and fine. 20 pcs.
567. Small copper size. Good and fine. 20 pcs.
568. Small copper size. Good and fine. 20 pcs.
569. Small copper size. Good and fine. 20 pcs.
570. Small copper size. Good and fine. 20 pcs.
571. Small copper size. Good and fine. 20 pcs.
572. Small copper size. Good and fine. 20 pcs.
573. Large size. Copper. Good and fine. 12 pcs.
574. Small size. Lead. Scarce. Good and fine. 10 pcs.
575. Small size. Odd lots. 8 pierced. 25 pcs.

Foreign Coins in Base Metal and Silver.

In the following collection of foreign base metal and silver coins, are many fine, rare and curious pieces, and the duplicates, if any, are such as naturally drift into a collection unnoticed. A curious and rare lot is that of the early South American Republics, many of which are very scarce, and lots 600, 603, 604, 608, 611 and 627 are very desirable. In the European silver and base metal, are many rare coins, and the set of Swiss and German small coins contains specimens of nearly all of this varied mintage.

Base Metal Coins.

576. Previous to 1700. Fair to fine. 9 pcs.

577. Previous to 1800.   Fair to fine.   10 pcs.
578. Previous to 1800.   Fair to fine.   10 pcs.
579. Previous to 1800.   Fair to fine.   10 pcs.
580. Previous to 1800.   Fair to fine.   10 pcs.
581. Previous to 1800.   Fair to fine.   10 pcs.
582. Previous to 1800.   Fair to fine.   10 pcs.
583. Previous to 1800.   Fair to fine.   10 pcs.
584. Previous to 1800.   Fair to fine.   10 pcs.
585. Since 1800.   Fair to fine.   20 pcs.
586. Since 1800.   Fair to fine.   20 pcs.
587. Since 1800.   Fair to fine.   20 pcs.
588. Since 1800.   Fair to fine.   20 pcs.
589. Since 1800.   Fair to fine.   20 pcs.
590. Since 1800.   Fair to fine.   20 pcs.
591. Since 1800.   Fair to fine.   20 pcs.
592. Since 1800.   Fair to fine.   20 pcs.
593. Turkish tin coins.   Curious lot.   Fine.   11 pcs.
594. Arabic tin coins.   Very curious lot.   Fine.   8 pcs.
595. Pierced coins.   A curious lot.   Good.   17 pcs.

Silver Coins.

SOUTH AMERICA.

596. 1818 and 1819.   Caracas mint.   Fine and good.   Face value, 75.   3 pcs.
597. 1849 and 1852.   Half dollars, Argentine Confederation.   Good.   2 pcs.
598. 1841 and 1855.   Ecuador half dollars.   1843 quarter.   Good and rare.
    3 pcs.
599. 1870.   Gautamala half dollar.   Fine.
600. 1835.   Colombia dollar.   Fine.
601. 1803 and 1835.   Colombia quarter dollars.   Fair and good.   3 pcs.
602. ¼, 1 and 2 reals and half dollar of Costa Rica.   Good.   Face, 95 cts.   5 pcs.
603. 1826.   Provinces La Plata dollar.   Very fine.   Rare.
604. 1821.   Colombia dollar.   Very good.   Rare.
605. 1839.   New Granada dollar.   Very good.   Rare.
606. Colombia.   Three one real and one two real pieces.   Good.   Face, 50
    cts.   4 pcs.
607. 1813.   Brazil, dollar size.   Fine.
608. 1816.   Brazil, dollar size.   Good.   Pierced.
609. 1819.   Brazil, dollar size.   Fine.
610. 1820.   Brazil, dollar size.   Fine.
611. 1824.   Brazil, dollar size.   Fine.
612. 1855.   Brazil, dollar size.   Fine, but pierced.
613. 1856.   Brazil, 1,000 and 200 reis pieces.   Fine.   Face, 60 cts.   2 pcs.
614. Chili.   Necessity dollar, I. P. and star on obverse.   Reverse blank.
    Fine and very rare.
615. 1874.   Chili, dollar size.   Good, but pierced.
616. 1875.   Chili, dollar size.   Fine.
617. 1875.   Chili, dollar size.   Fine.
618. 1876.   Chili, dollar size.   Fine.
619. 1876.   Chili, dollar size.   Fine.
620. 1877.   Chili, dollar size.   Fine.
621. Chili.   Small coins.   Fine.   Face $1.20.   7 pcs.
622. 1840.   Bolivia, dollar size.   Bust of Bolivar.   Uncirculated.
623. 1845.   Bolivia, dollar size.   Bust of Bolivar.   Fine.
624. 1859.   Bolivia, dollar size.   Bust of Bolivar.   Uncirculated.
625. 1830.   Bolivia, half dollars.   Bust of Bolivar.   Fine.   2 pcs.
626. Small coins of Bolivia.   Good and fine.   Face, 60 cts.   4 pcs.
627. 1837.   Peru, Cazco mint.   Rare device.   Dollar.   Fine, but pierced.

628. 1838. Peru, dollar size. Fine. Scarce.
629. 1842. Peru, dollar size. Fine. Scarce.
630. 1866. Peru, dollar size. Present mintage. Fine.
631. 1869. Peru, dollar size. Present mintage. Fine.
632. 1872. Peru, dollar size. Present mintage. Fine.
633. 1838 and 1842. Peru, half dollars. Good. 2 pcs.
634. Small coins of Peru. Fine to uncirculated. Face, 75 cts. 11 pcs.
635. 1842. Mexico, dollar. Fair.
636. 1845. Mexico, dollar. Fair.
637. 1870. Mexico, dollar. Fine.
638. 1871. Mexico, dollar. Good.
639. 1872. Mexico, dollar. Good.
640. 1873. Mexico, dollar. Good.
641. 1873. Mexico, dollar. Uncirculated.
642. 1874. Mexico, dollar. Fine.
643. 1876. Mexico. Dollar. Fine.
644. 1877. Mexico. Dollar. Fine.
645. 1877. Mexico. Dollar. Uncirculated.
646. 1878. Mexico. Dollar. Fine.
647. 1878. Mexico. Dollar. Fine.
648. 1850 and 1852. Mexico. Half dollars. Good. 2 pcs.
649. 1878. Mexico. Half dollar. Uncirculated.
650. Mexico. Quarter dollars. Good. 4 pcs.
651. Mexico. Quarter dollars. Good. 4 pcs.
652. Mexico. Quarter dollars. Good and fine. 3 pcs.
653. Mexico. Small coins. Good and fine. Face, 60 cts. 8 pcs.
654. 1866. Mexico. Maximilian dollar. Fine.
655. 1866. Mexico. Maximilian half dollar. Fine.
656. Pierced coins. Face, 75 cts. 10 pcs.
657. Odd coins. Good and rare. Face, 35 cts. 3 pcs.

Spanish Silver.

658. 1788. Dollar. Carolus III. Good.
659. 1791. Dollar. Carolus IV. Good.
660. 1795. Dollar. Carolus IV. Good.
661. 1806. Dollar. Carolus IV. Good. Pierced.
662. 1808. Dollar. Carolus IV. Good.
663. 1811. Dollar. Ferdinand VII. Fine.
664. 1814. Dollar. Ferdinand VII. Good.
665. 1871. Dollar. Amadeo I. Good and scarce, but pierced.
666. 1875. Dollar. Alfonso XII. Fine, but scratched on obverse.
667. 1876. Carolus III. Half dollar. Good.
668. Early. Quarter dollar. Fair to fine. 5 pcs.
669. Carolus III. quarter dollars. Fair to fine. 4 pcs.
669a. Carolus III. and IV. quarter dollars. Good to fine. 4 pcs.
670. Carolus III. quarter dollars. Good to fine. 5 pcs.
671. Ferdinand VII. quarter dollars. Good and fine. 2 pcs.
672. Philip V. five and ten cents. Good and rare. 2 pcs.
673. Necessity coins and real of Joseph Bonaparte. 2 pierced, fair and good.
     4 pcs.
674. Cob money. Curious, 5 pierced, weight about $1.00. 13 pcs.
675. Pillar and other early small coins. Face, 55 cts. Good. 5 pcs.
676. Carolus and Ferdinand small coins. Face $1.50. Fair to fine. 15 pcs.
677. Coins of the republic of 1869. Face $1.40. Fine. 4 pcs.
678. Coins of Isabella. Face, 70 cts. Good to fine. 5 pcs.

French Silver.

679. 1731. Louis XV. Young head. Crown. Fair. Scarce.

680. 1765. Louis XV. Old head. Crown. Good.
681. First republic. 5 francs. Hercules and female figure. Good. Scarce.
682. 1814. Napoleon I., last coinage. Bust of Emperor. 5 francs. Fine. Rare.
683. 1819. Louis XVIII. 5 francs. Very fair.
684. 1823. Louis XVIII. 5 francs. Fine.
685. 1844. Louis Philippe 5 francs. Fine.
686. 1845. Louis Philippe 5 francs. Good.
687. 1846. Louis Philippe. 5 francs. Fine.
688. 1849. Republic. Hercules and female figures. 5 francs. Very fine. Scarce.
689. Henry III. Testoon. Coat of Arms. Poor. Rare.
690. Louis XIV. Good demi-franc. Louis XV. Poor half crown. Good testoon. 3 pcs.
691. Napoleon I., ¼, ½, 1 and 2 francs for France and Italy. Fair and good. Face. 95 cts. 6 pcs.
692. Later coins of France. Fair to fine. 2 pierced. Face, $1.85. 19 pcs.

Italian Silver.

693. 1800. Sicily. Ferdinand III. Bust. Dollar size. Good. Scarce.
694. 1769, 1794, 1796. Busts of Kings of Sardinia. Good. Face, 60. 3 pcs.
695. Coins of Victor Emanuel. Fine and uncirculated. Face, $1.45. 10 pcs.
696. 1808. Accolated busts of Eliza Bonaparte and husband. Good. Franc. Scarce.
697. 1845. Lire of Tuscany. Good.
698. 1780. Pius VI. Bust. Reverse, Virgin Mary. Lire. Good.
699. 5 Baiocchi of Pius VI. and Pius IX. Pontifical Arms. Fair and fine. 2 pcs.
700. 1853. 50 Baiocchi of Pius IX. Bust. Good and scarce, but pierced.
701. 1866. 2 Lire of Pius IX. Bust. Fine. Scarce.
702. **Holland.** William II. Dollar size. Very fine. Scarce.
703. " William III. Dollar size. Very fine.
704. " Small coins. Fair to fine. Face, 65 cts. 10 pcs.
705. **Belgium.** 1852. Leopold. 5 francs. Fine.
706. " Small coins. Good and fine. Face, 55 cts. 4 pcs.
707. **Prussia.** 1840. Bust of Frederic William III. Reverse, beautiful draped coat of arms. A double thaler. A large, well-struck and rare coin. Face, $1.50. Very fine.
708. **Prussia.** William IV. 5 mark or dollar. Fine.
709. " Coins of Frederick the Great. Fair and good. Face, 75. 3 pcs.
710. " Coins of Frederick William III. Fair and good. Face, $2.00. 10 pcs.
711. **Prussia.** Coins of William IV. Fine. Face, 55 cts. 2 pcs.
712. " Minor silver coins. Fine. Face, 85 cts. 8 pcs.

German States, Silver.

713. 1753. St. Martin dividing his cloak with a beggar. Reverse, coat of arms. Very good, indeed, for this rare crown.
714. 1856. Double Thaler. Obverse, bust of Maximilian II., of Bavaria. Reverse, Exposition building. Struck in commemoration of the exposition of 1856, at Maine. Good. Rare.
715. 1796. Lubeck. 32 schilling. Dollar size. Good and rare, but pierced.
716. 1831. Ernst August, King of Hanover. Thaler. Good. Scarce.
717. 1831. Hanover. Rampant horse. Half dollar size. Uncirculated.
718. 1790. Brunswick. Rampant horse. Half dollar size. Good. Scarce.
719. 1791. Brunswick. Half dollar size. Fine.
720. 1765. Mark of Maria Theresa, and mark of her husband, Francis. A very good pair. Face, 40 cts. 2 pcs.

721. Mixed German coins. Fair to good. Previous to 1700. Face, $1.00. 8 pes.
722. Mixed German coins. Fair to good. Previous to 1700. Face, 20. 2 pes.
723. Mixed German coins. Fair to good. Previous to 1700. Face, 20. 2 pes.
724. Mixed German coins. Fair to good. Previous to 1700. Face, 35 cts. 3 pes.
725. Mixed German coins. Good to fine. Previous to 1800. Face $1.00. 6 pes.
726. Mixed German coins. Good to fine. Previous to 1800. Face, 70 cts. 5 pes.
727. Mixed German coins. Fair and good. Previous to 1800. Face, 60 cts. 5 pes.
728. Mixed German coins. Good and fine. Since 1800. Face, 83 cts. 8 pes.
729. Mixed German coins. Uncirculated. Since 1800. Face, 30 cts. 2 pes.

Sweden, Norway and Denmark, Silver.

730. 1699 and 1775. Dime size. Good and rare. 2 pes.
731. Monograms. Fine and uncirculated. Face, 75 cts. 5 pes.
732. Coats of arms. Good. 1 pierced. Face, 35 cts. 3 pes.
733. Portraits. Good, fine and uncirculated. Face, 65 cts. 5 pes.
734. Portraits. Carl XV. Uncirculated. Beautiful. Face. 30. 2 pes.
735. **Russia.** 10, 20, 25 and 50 Kopecs. Uncirculated and a beautiful set. Face $1.05. 4 pes.
736. **Russia.** 5, 10, 15 and 20 Kopecs. Fine. Face. 56 cts. 4 pes.
737. **Japan.** 5, 10, 20 and 50 cents. one dollar. A beautiful, uncirculated set of the modern coinage. Face $1.85. 5 pes.
738. **Japan.** Itzebue. Oblong square. Fine. Rare.
739. **Japan.** Quarter itzebues. 1 pierced. Fine. Rare. 2 pes.
740. **Japan.** Curious dump coin of base metal. Old and rare. About the size of a Siam Tical. Stamped characters.
741. **Siam.** Tical. Dump. Rare.
742. **Turkey and Greece.** Very fine. Face, 25 cts. 3 pes.
743. **Portugal.** Good. Old. Face, 15 cts. 2 pes.
744. **Denmark.** 1757, 1764, 1767. Obverse. Monograms. Reverse. Ship sailing. Coins struck for the Danish-American colonies. Fair and good. Face about, 50 cts. Rare. 3 pes.
745. **German Empire.** 1 pfenning to 1 mark. A representative set in copper, nickel and silver, in very fine condition. Face. 80 cts. 7 pes.

Swiss Base and Silver Coins.

746. 1622. Base. Fair and fine. Rare. 2 pes.
747. 1710, 1726, 1727, 1740. Base. Good. Rare. 4 pes.
748. 1789, 1798, 1799. Base. Good and fine. Rare. 4 pes.
749. No dates. Early coinage. Base. Good. Rare. 2 pes.
750. Canton Argau. Base. Good and fine. 5 pes.
751. Canton Appenzel. Silver. Base. 1 batz. 1 pe.
752. Canton Basel. Base. Good and fine. 4 pes.
753. Canton Berne. Silver. 1826. 2½ batz. Fine. 1 pe.
754. Canton Berne. Base. Good and fine. 6 pes.
755. Canton Geneva. Base. Good to uncirculated. 5 pes.
756. Canton Geneva. Base. Good to uncirculated. 5 pes.
757. Canton Geneva. Base. Good to fine. 5 pes.
758. Canton Glarus. Base. Good. 2 pes.
759. Canton Gran Brunden. Base. Fine. 2 pes.
760. Canton Freyburg. Base. Good and fine. 5 pes.
761. Canton Lucerne. Silver. Fine. Face, 30 cts. 3 pes.
762. Canton Lucerne. Base. Good and fine. 6 pes.
763. Canton Neuchatel. Base. Good and fine. 8 pes.

764. Canton Schwyz. Base. Good and fine. 3 pcs.
765. Canton Soldthurn. Base. Good and fine. 4 pcs.
766. Canton St. Gallen. Base. Good and fine. 8 pcs.
767. Canton St. Gallen. Silver. Good. Rare. Face, 40 cts. 2 pcs.
768. Canton Thurgau. Base. Good. 1 pc.
769. Canton Tiano. Base. Good. 3 pcs.
770. Canton Vaud. Silver. Fine. Face, 20 cts. 1 pc.
771. Canton Vaud. Base. Fine. 1 pc.
772. Canton Zurich. Base. Good. 2 pcs.
773. Republican Confederation. Silver. Face, 60 cts. Fine. 4 pcs.
774. Republican Confederation. Base. Previous to 1800. Fine and rare. 5 pcs.
775. Republican Confederation. Base. 1800 to 1843. Fine and scarce. 4 pcs.
776. Republican Confederation. Late coinage. 1 to 20 rappen. Good to uncirculated. 8 pcs.

English Silver.

777. Ethelred II. Penny. Fine. Rare.
778. Henry I. Penny. Fair. Rare.
779. Henry II. Penny. Fine. Scarce.
780. Henry III. Penny. Fine.
781. Henry III. Pennies. Duplicates. 2 pcs.
782. Edward I. Penny. Good.
783. Edward I. Pennies. Good duplicates. 2 pcs.
784. Edward II. Penny. Good.
785. Edward III. Groat. Fine. Pierced.
786. Richard II. Half penny. Good. Rare.
787. Henry IV. Penny. Fine. Scarce.
788. Henry V. Groat. Fine. Scarce.
789. Henry VI. Penny. Good. Scarce.
790. Edward IV. Groat. Fair. Pierced.
791. Richard III. Penny. Fair. Rare.
792. Henry VII. Penny. Fair. Rare.
793. Henry VIII. Groat. First coinage. Profile to right. Very fine. Rare.
794. Henry VIII. Groat. For Ireland. Fair. Pierced. Rare.
795. Edward VI. Shilling. Very good indeed, but pierced.
796. Elizabeth shilling. Obverse fair. Reverse good.
797. James I. shilling. Good.
798. Charles I. shilling. Hammered. Good.
799. Charles I. Penny and two penny pieces. Fair. Rare. 2 pcs.
800. Charles II. Three pence. 1679. Good.
801. James II. Penny. 1684. Fair.
802. William and Mary. Half crown. 1689. Good.
803. William III. Sixpence. 1697. Good.
804. Anne. Shilling. 1708. Fine.
805. George I. Four pence. 1727. Good.
806. George II. Six pence. 1737. Good.
807. George III. Crown. 1819. Good. Obverse Bust. Reverse St. George.
808. George III. Bank of England dollar. 1804. Fine. Scarce.
809. George III. Bank token for three shillings. 1812. Fine. Rare.
810. George III. Half crown, shillings, and sixpences. Face, $1.32. Fair to fine. 5 pcs.
811. George IV. Half crowns. 1820 and 1823. Varieties. Good. 2 pcs.
812. George IV. Shilling and sixpence. 1824, 1826. Good. 2 pcs.
813. George IV. Colonials. Face, 30. 4 pcs.
814. William IV. Rupee. 1835. Fine. Scarce.

815. William IV. Shilling. 1834. Fine.
816. Victoria. Crown. 1844. Fine.
817. Victoria. Crown. 1845. Fine.
818. Victoria. Hong Kong dollar. 1868. Fine. Rare.
819. Victoria. Half crown and florin. Good. Face, $1.05. 2 pcs.
820. Victoria. Florins. Good and fine. 2 pcs.
82!. Victoria. Rupee. 1862. Fine.
822. Victoria. Shillings. Fine. 2 pcs.
823. Victoria and William IV. Small silver. Face. 64 cts. Fine. 9 pcs.
824. Victoria. Canada. Good and fine. Face, $1.00. Fine. 6 pcs.
825. Victoria. Good and fine. Face, $1.00. 7 pcs.
826. Victoria. Good and fine. Face, $1.00. 2 pcs.
827. Victoria. Small colonials. India, Hong Kong, etc. Face. 30 cts. Good. 5 pcs.
828. Maunday money. William and Mary to Victoria. Good and fine. 1 pierced. Face, 46 cts. 7 pcs.

Washington Medals.

Battle series. Obverse, bust of Washington in circle of stars, date 1876. Below, Legend, "The Centennial Year of our National Independence." Reverse, blazing star enclosing date 1876. Name of battle above, number and date below, all enclosed in a wreath of oak leaves. White metal. Size 22.
829. No. 1. Moore's creek. North Carolina.
830. No. 2. Sullivan's Island. South Carolina.
831. No. 3. Long Island. New York.
832. No. 4. Harlem Plains. New York.
833. No. 5. Lake Champlain. New York.
834. No. 6. White Plains. New York.
835. No. 7. Fort Washington. New York.
836. No. 8. Trenton. New Jersey.
837. A duplicate set. 8 pcs.
838. Large bust of Washington. Reverse, first in war, etc. Date of birth and death. In commemoration of 100 anniversary of American Independence. Gilt proof. Size 27.
839. Duplicate in W. M. proof.
840. Washington. Reverse, liberty bell. W. M. proof. Size 24.
841. Washington. Reverse, Masonic symbols. W. M. proof. Size 32.
842. Washington. Reverse, dedicated to children of America. W. M. proof. Size 22. 2 pcs.
843. Washington. Reverse. Independence Hall. W. M. proof. Size 24.
844. Washington. Different reverses. W. M. fair to proof. Size 10 to 16. 5 pcs.
845. Washington. Merriam's card. Fine. Size 17.
846. Washington. Great central fair. Copper and brass. Uncirculated. Size 12. 2 pcs.
847. Washington. Idler's card. Silvered. Uncirculated. Size 22.
848. Washington. Idler's card. Copper. Uncirculated. Size 22.
849. Washington. Brimlow's cards. Copper and brass. Uncirculated. Size 15. 2 pcs.
849a. Washington. Brimlow's cards. Copper and Brass. Uncirculated. Size 12 and 15. 3 pcs.
850. Washington. Mason and Sage's cards. W. M. Uncirculated. Size 12 and 15. 2 pcs.
851. Washington. 1861 to 1864. Tokens. Good to fine. Size 12. 7 pcs.
851a. Washington. 1861 to 1864. Tokens. Good to fine. Size 12. 5 pcs.
852. Washington. Spielmarks. Good to fine. 10 pcs.

852a. Washington. Spielmarks. Good to fine. 4 pcs.
853. Washington. Reverse. Martha Washington. Size 11 and 18. Proofs. 3 pcs.
854. Washington. Reverse : Sword, fasces and wreath lying on a draped altar. Date 1797 below. "Commission resigned. Presidency relinquished." Copper cast silvered. Copy of a rare medal. Good. Size 26.
855. Washington. Reverse : Born Feb. 22, 1732. Died Dec. 14. 1799. Bronze proof. Size 20.
856. Washington. Reverse : Baltimore monument. North Point celebration. Bronze proof. Size 20.
857. Washington. Reverse : Time increases his fame. Bronze. Fine. Size 18.
858. Washington, with loop, size 14. Success to U. S. Scalloped. Good. 2 pcs.

Miscellaneous Medals and Jetons.

859. Medal of the World's Fair in New York. 1853. Battered on the edge, but good. Bronze. Size 36.
860. Centennial medal in honor of Catholic visitors, by Loubenheimer. Bust of Pius IX. W. M. proof. Size 28.
861. Centennial medal in honor of French visitors. Bust of Marshall McMahon. W. M. proof. Size 28.
862. Centennial medal. View of the signing of the Declaration of Independence. W. M. proof. Size 32.
863. Centennial medal. View of the Main Building. W. M. proof. Size 27.
864. Odd Fellows' Hall, New York. By Lovett. W. M. proof. Size 27.
865. Sunday-school reward medal, and Union Reform Association. W. M. proofs. Size 20 and 22. 2 pcs.
866. Obverse, John Bull and Brother Jonathan. Ocean and steamship between. Congratulations in the field. Reverse, Atlantic Telegraph successfully laid, 5th of August, 1858. W. M. Fine. Size 20.
867. Abraham Lincoln. Reverse, broken column. W. M. proof. Size 32.
868. Medal of the Grand Army. W. M. proof. Size 32.
869. Medal of the centennial of the massacre in Fort Grisnold, Conn. Arnold's raid. Obverse, Plan of the fort where the massacre took place. Reverse, two continental soldiers in the corner of a parapet, defending the same. Appropriate inscriptions. Bronze. But 250 struck in this medal, and rare. Size 26.
870. A duplicate in W. M. proof. Scarce.
871. Political medals of Fillmore. Lincoln, Johnson, Grant and Garfield, in W. M. Different sizes. Good to proof. 8 pcs.
872. Political medals of Jackson, Fillmore, Pierce. Sumner, Hancock. Garfield and Arthur, in brass. Good to proof. Different sizes. 7 pcs.
873. Political medalets of Jackson, Harrison, Taylor and Lincoln, in copper. Different sizes. Fair to fine. 5 pcs.
874. Lafayette. Bust. Reverse, struck in commemoration of his visit to the U. S. in 1824. Bronze. Fine. Size 30.
875. A duplicate. Has been in the fire. Fair.
876. Bust of Gregory XIII. Reverse, scene emblematic of the massacre of St. Bartholomew. Robert Morris' copy of this rare medal. Proof, rare. Bronze. Size 20.
877. Henry IV. and Louis XVIII. of France. Busts jugata. Fine. Bronze. Size 20.
878. Charles X. of France. Bust. Reverse, inscription. Bronze. Fine. Size 20.
879. Louis Philippe of France. Bust. Reverse, inscription. Bronze. Good. Size 17.

880. Louis Napoleon. Bust. Reverse, three figures. For the exposition of 1855. Bronze. Good. Size 32.
880a. Exposition building of 1855. Reverse as above. A presentation medal. W. M. bronzed. Good. Size 32.
881. Louis Napoleon. Bust. Reverse, exposition building of 1861. Gilt bronze. Proof. Size 23.
882. Louis Napoleon. Bust. Reverse inscription, Plebiate of 1851. Proof. Bronze. Scarce. Size 22.
883. Looped medalets of Louis Napoleon and his son, and of Louis Napoleon and Victor Emanuel. Good and fine. Size 15. 3 pcs.
884. Looped medalets of Napoleon I. Duke of Orleans, etc. Fine. 3 pcs.
885. Jetons of Napoleon I., Alexander I. of Russia, Louis XVIII., and Louis Napoleon. Fine. One pierced. 4 pcs.
886. Charm medalets with rings, of Napoleon III., Prince Jerome, Eugene Bucharnois, Eugenie, and Victor Emanuel. Fine. 5 pcs.
887. Jetons of George IV. William IV. and Queen Adelaide, Victoria and Albert. Good and fine. 4 pcs.

Roman Bronze.

888. Pompey the Great. Double head. Reverse, prow of a ship. 2 bronze. Fair.
889. Julius Caesar. Bust. Reverse, bust of Augustus. 1 bronze. Good. Rare.
890. Augustus Caesar. Bust. Reverse, S. C. 2 bronze. Very good.
891. Augustus Caesar. Bust. Reverse, temple. 2 bronze. Fair.
892. Tiberius. Bust. Reverse, rod of health. 2 bronze. Fair.
893. Caligula. Emperor, with female figures in temple. Reverse, Pietas. 1 bronze. Good.
894. Caligula. Bust. Reverse, Vesta. 2 bronze. Fair.
895. Antonia. Bust. Reverse, seated figure. 1 bronze. Poor. Rare.
896. Claudius. Bust. Reverse, Mars. 2 bronze. Fair.
896a. Claudius. Bust. Reverse, Mars. 2 bronze. Good.
897. Nero. Bust. Reverse. Neptune. 2 bronze. Good.
898. Nero. Bust. Reverse, Augustus, Potin, Alexandrian. 2 bronze. Fine. Very rare.
899. Nero. Bust. Reverse, port of Ostia. 1 bronze. Fine. Paduan.
900. Galba. Bust. Reverse, emperor addressing soldiers. 1 bronze. Fine. Paduan.
901. Otho. Bust. Reverse, emperor addressing soldiers. Pierced. 1 bronze. Good. Paduan.
902. Vitellius. Bust. Reverse, clasped hands. 2 bronze. Fair. Rare.
903. Vespasian. Bust. Reverse, figure seated. 2 bronze. Good. Rare.
904. Titus. Bust. Reverse, figure seated. 2 bronze. Good.
905. Titus. Emperor seated. Reverse, coliseum. 1 bronze. Fair. Rare.
906. Domitian. Bust. Reverse, emperor standing. 1 bronze. Good. Rare.
907. Domitian. Bust. Reverse, figure of Abundance. 2 bronze. Fair.
908. Nerva. Bust. Reverse. Fortuna. 1 bronze. Very good. Rare.
909. Trajan. Bust. Reverse, emperor seated. 1 bronze. Fair.
910. Trajan. Bust. Reverse, Fortuna. 2 bronze. Fair.
911. Hadrian. Bust. Reverse, Hilaritis. 1 bronze. Fine.
912. Sabina. Bust. Reverse, Constantia. 1 bronze. Very fair. Rare.
913. Antoninus Pius. Bust. Reverse, standing figure. 1 bronze. Good.
914. Faustina Senior. Bust. Reverse, Justitia. 2 bronze. Fair.
915. Marcus Aurelius. Bust. Reverse, Liberality. 1 bronze. Good.
916. Marcus Aurelius. Bust. Reverse, Africa. 2 bronze. Good. Rare.
917. Faustina Junior. Bust. Reverse, figure with children. 1 bronze. Fair. Rare.

918. Faustina Junior. Bust. Reverse, figure standing. 2 bronze. Fair.
919. Lucilla. Bust. Reverse, seated figure. 1 bronze. Fair.
920. Commodus. Bust. Reverse, Justice. 1 bronze. Fair. Rare.
921. Crispina. Bust. Reverse, standing figure. 2 bronze. Good. Rare.
922. Pertina. Bust. Reverse, figure and globe. 1 bronze. Fine, but a
     Padnan.
923. Didius Julianus. Bust. Reverse, abundance. 3 bronze. Fine, but a
     Becker.
924. Albinus. Bust Reverse, Justice. 1 bronze. Good. Rare.
925. Septimus Severus. Bust. Reverse, soldier and trophy. 1 bronze.
     Fine. Rare.
926. Septimus Severus. Bust. Reverse, Victory. 2 bronze. Good. Green
     patina.
927. Caracalla. Bust. Reverse, Justice. 1 bronze. Fair. Rare.
928. Caracalla. Bust. Reverse, flaming altar. 2 bronze. Good. Rare.
     Greek.
928a. Macrinus. Bust. Reverse, figure. 2 bronze. Very good. Very rare.
929. Elagabalus. Bust. Reverse, eagle. 2 bronze. Fine. Rare. Greek.
930. Alexander Severus. Bust. Reverse, Victory, 1 bronze. Reverse, eagle,
     2 bronze. Good. 2 pcs.
931. Maximianus, the Giant. Bust. Reverse, Felix Augusta. 1 bronze.
     Fine. Rare.
932. Balbinus. Bust. Reverse, figure standing. 1 bronze. Good. Rare.
933. Pupienus. Bust. Reverse, figure standing. 1 bronze. Fair. Rare.
934. Gordian III. Bust. Reverse, Eternity. 1 bronze. Good.
935. Philip I. Bust. Reverse, 1 bronze, Liberality. 2 bronze. Good. 2 pcs.
936. Otacilia. Bust. Reverse, Concordia. Fine. 1 bronze.
937. Philip II. Bust. 1st and 2d bronze. Good. 2 pcs.
938. Trajanus Decius. Bust. Reverse, figure and standards. Good.
939. Gallus, and Hostilianus. 2 bronze. Very fair. 2 pcs.
940. Volusianus. 1 bronze, Valerian. 2 bronze. Good. Rare. 2 pcs.
941. Gallienus, Salonina, Victorinus, Tetricus Jun, and Claudius Gothicus. 3
     bronze. Good. 5 pcs.
942. Quintillius, Aurelian and Severina. 3 bronze. Good. 3 pcs.
943. Tacitus and Probus. 3 bronze. Good. 3 pcs.
944. Carinus, Carus and Diocletian. 3 bronze. Fair and good. 3 pcs.
945. Diocletian, Maximianus Hercules and Constantius Chlorus. 2 bronze.
     Fine. 3 pcs.
946. Galerius, Maximus Daza and Maxentius. Fine. 2 bronze. 3 pcs.
947. Diocletian, Licinius I. and II. Good and fine. 3 bronze. 4 pcs.
948. Constantine I. Crispus, Constantine II., Constantius II. and Constans,
     and City of Constantinople. Very good and fine. 3 bronze. 6 pcs.
949. Constantine I., Constantius II., Magnentius, Constans, Constantius
     Gallus. 1 pierced, fair to fine. 5 pcs.
950. Julian, the Philosopher. Reverse, bull. 1 pierced. 1 bronze. Fair
     and good. 2 pcs.
951. Julian, the Philosopher. Jovian, Valentinian I., Valens and Gratian.
     Fair to fine. 3 bronze. 5 pcs.
952. Valentinian II., Theodosius I., Arcadius. Fine lot. 4 pcs.
953. John Zimisces and a Byzantine. Fine lot. 2 pcs.
954. First bronze of various emperors. Poor to good. 5 pcs.
955. First bronze of various emperors. Poor to good. 5 pcs.
956. Second bronze of various emperors. Poor to good. 10 pcs.
957. Second bronze of various emperors. Poor to good. 10 pcs.
958. Third bronze of various emperors. Poor to good. 20 pcs.
959. Third bronze of various emperors. Poor to good. 20 pcs.
960. Third bronze of various emperors. Poor to good. 25 pcs.
961. Third bronze of various emperors. Poor to good. 25 pcs.

Becker's Copies, Silvered, of Very Rare Coins.

962. Alexander the Great. Tetradrachm.
963. Antiochus I. Tetradrachm.
964. Antiochus II. Tetradrachm.
965. Antiochus III. Tetradrachm.
966. Antiochus IV. Tetradrachm.
967. Prusia. Tetradrachm.
968. Demetrius II. Tetradrachm.
969. Acanthus. Tetradrachm.
970. Head of Minerva. Reverse, Hercules strangling lion. Tetradrachm.
971. Bacchus. Reverse, bull. Tetradrachm.

U. S. Silver Coins.

972. **Three Cent Pieces.** 1851, 1852, 1853, 1854. Good and fine. 8 pcs.
973. 1855. Fine. Very scarce.
974. 1856 to 1862 inclusive. Good and fine. 10 pcs.
975. 1859, 1860, 1861, 1862. Uncirculated. 4 pcs.
976. 1863. Uncirculated. Mint bloom. Rare.
977. 1864. Uncirculated. Mint bloom. Rare.
978. 1865. Uncirculated. Mint bloom. Rare.
979. 1866. Uncirculated. Rare.
980. 1867. Proof. Rare.
981. 1868. Proof. Rare.
982. 1869. Proof. Rare.
983. 1870. Uncirculated. Scarce.
984. 1871. Proof. Scarce.
985. 1872. Fine. Scarce.
986. 1872. Proof. Scarce.
987. **Half Dimes.** 1794. Altered date. 1795 good. 2 pcs.
988. 1796 poor and pierced, but date strong. 1797. Battered. Date strong. 2 pcs.
989. 1800. Fair. Battered. 1801, poor and pierced. Date visible. 2 pcs.
990. 1803. Battered, but fair. Rare.
991. 1829, 1832, '33, '34, '35, '37, starless, '38, '39 O. Mint. Good and fine. 7 pcs.
992. 1840 Draped. 1844 P. and O. Mints. Fair and good. 4 pcs.
993. 1853 with and without arrows. 1854 and 1857. Fine and uncirculated. 4 pcs.
994. 1860. P. and O. Mints. 1861, 1862. Fine and uncirculated. 4 pcs.
995. 1863. Uncirculated. Rare.
996. 1864. Uncirculated. Rare.
997. 1865. Uncirculated. Rare.
998. 1866. Uncirculated. Rare.
999. 1867. Uncirculated. Scarce.
1000. 1867. Uncirculated. Scarce.
1001. 1868. Uncirculated. Scarce.
1002. 1869. Uncirculated. Scarce.
1003. 1865. Good. 1870, '71, '72, '73. Fine. 5 pcs.
1004. **Dimes.** 1796. Pierced and plugged. Good. Scarce.
1004a. 1796. Fair and good. Both pierced. Scarce. 2 pcs.
1005. 1797. Fair, pierced. Rare.
1006. 1798. Fair. Scarce.
1007. 1800. Poor and fair, the former pierced. Scarce. 2 pcs.
1008. 1801. Poor. Dates visible. Rare. 2 pcs.
1009. 1802. Battered but fair. Rare.
1010. 1803. Battered but fair. Rare.
1011. 1803. Battered, fair. 1 pierced. Rare. 2 pcs.
1012. 1805. Fair. Scarce.

1013. 1807. Fair. Scarce.
1014. 1809. Fair. Scarce.
1015. 1811 over 1809. Good for date. Scarce.
1016. 1811. Fair. Scarce.
1017. 1822. Very good for date. Rare.
1018. 1823, '24, '25, '27, '29. Good and fine. 6 pcs.
1019. 1830, '31, '32, '33, '34, '35, '37. Fine and very fine. 7 pcs.
1020. 1844. Very good indeed. Scarce.
1021. 1846. Fine. Rare.
1022. 1863. Uncirculated. Scarce.
1023. 1864. Uncirculated. Scarce.
1024. 1865. Uncirculated. Scarce.
1025. 1865. Uncirculated. Scarce.
1026. 1867. Uncirculated. Scarce.
1027. 1867. Uncirculated. Scarce.
1028. 1879. Uncirculated. Scarce.
1029. **Twenty Cent Piece.** 1875. S. Mint. Scarce. Fine.
1030. **Quarter Dollars.** 1796. Date strong. Very fair.
1031. 1796. Good. But has been pierced and plugged.
1032. 1796. Poor, but date good. Pierced.
1033. 1806 and 1807. Fair and good. 2 pcs.
1034. 1850 and 1851. Fair and good. 2 pcs.
1035. 1879. Uncirculated. Scarce.
1036. 1881. Uncirculated. Scarce.
1037. **Half Dollars.** 1794. Very good. Scratched on obverse. Rare.
1038. 1795. Very fair, but pierced.
1039. 1801. Very good indeed. Nearly fine. Rare.
1040. 1801. Good but pierced.
1041. 1802. Fine for this very rare date. Nicked.
1042. 1803. Fine.
1043. 1803. Fine.
1044. 1805. Fine. Nicks on obverse.
1045. 1805. Good.
1046. 1806. Pointed 6. Fine.
1047. 1806. Pointed 6. Very good.
1048. 1806. Pointed 6. Very good.
1049. 1807. Head to right. Fine.
1050. 1807. Head to left. Very fine.
1051. 1808. Very fine.
1052. 1809. Very fine.
1053. 1810. Fine.
1054. 1811. Very fine.
1055. 1813. Very fine.
1056. 1815. Very good for this rare date, but Aug. 1, 46 stamped on obverse field.
1057. 1817. Very fine.
1058. 1818. Very fine.
1059. 1818 over 1817. Good and scarce.
1060. 1819. Small date. Fine.
1061. 1820. Small date. Fine.
1062. 1821. Very fine.
1063. 1822. Very fine.
1064. 1823. Broken back 3. Fine. Scarce.
1065. 1824. Very fine.
1066. 1825. Very fine.
1067. 1826. Very fine.
1068. 1827. Very fine.
1069. 1829. Very fine.

1070. 1830. Very fine.
1071. 1831. Very fine.
1072. 1832. Very fine.
1073. 1833. Very fine.
1074. 1834. Very fine.
1075. 1835. Very fine.
1076. 1836. Very fine.
1077. 1837. Very fine.
1078. 1838. Very fine.
1079. 1839. Very fine. Head.
1080. 1839. Fine. Liberty seated. Drapery below elbow. Scarce.
1081. 1843. Very fine.
1082. 1844. Very fine.
1083. 1850. O. Mint. Fine. Scarce.
1084. 1851. O. Mint. Fine. Scarce.
1085. 1864. Very fine. Scarce.
1086. 1865. Very fine. Scarce.
1087. 1879. Uncirculated. Scarce.
1088. **Dollars.** 1795. Flowing hair. Dash behind head. Very good.
1089. 1795. Fillet head. Very good.
1090. 1796. Small date. Good, but scratched.
1091. 1797. Six stars facing. Good.
1092. 1797. Seven stars facing. Good.
1093. 1800. Plain date. Fine.
1094. 1846. Fine.
1095. 1847. Uncirculated.
1096. 1848. Very good. Scarce.
1097. 1849. Fine.
1098. 1853. Good.
1099. 1853. Very good.
1100. 1860. O. Mint. Fine. Scarce.
1101. 1864. Very good. Scarce.
1102. 1866. Fine. Scarce.
1103. 1868. Uncirculated. Scarce.
1104. 1871. Very fine. Scarce.
1105. 1871. Very fine. Scarce.
1106. 1873. Old style. Fine. Scarce.
1107. 1877. Trade. S. Mint. Uncirculated. Scarce.
1108. 1878. Trade. S. Mint. Uncirculated. Scarce.
1109. **Half Cents.** 1793. Very good. Scarce.
1110. 1794. Good. Scarce.
1111. 1795. Very fair.
1112. 1796. Electrotype. Good.
1113. 1797. Very fair indeed. Obverse good. Scarce.
1114. 1800. Very fair indeed. Obverse good. Scarce.
1115. 1802. Fair only. Rare.
1116. 1803 to 1809. Good to fine. 1806 pierced. 7 pcs.
1117. 1810. Good, but scratched. Scarce.
1118. 1811. Very fair. Rare.
1119. 1825, 1826, 1828, 1829. Good and fine. 4 pcs.
1120. 1832, 1833, 1834, 1835. Good and fine. 4 pcs.
1121. 1849, 1850, 1851. Good and fine. 3 pcs.
1122. 1853 to 1857 inclusive. Good and fine. Star stamped on 1857. 5 pcs.
1123. 1793 poor indeed. 1795 very fair. 1796 electrotype. 3 pcs.
1124. 1797 and 1800. Fair. 2 pes.
1125. 1803, 1805, 1807, 1809. Fair to fine. 7 pcs.
1126. 1810 and 1811. Very fair. Scarce. 2 pcs.
1127. 1826, 1828, 1829. two pierced. Good. 4 pcs.

1128. 1832, 1833, 1834. Good. 4 pcs.
1129. 1853, 1856. Good. 3 pcs.
1130 **Cents.** 1793 Liberty cap. Edge scalloped. Fair. Rare.
1131. 1794, '95, '96, '97, '98. Fair. 5 pcs.
1132. 1799. Poor, but I think genuine.
1133. 1800 and 1801. Varieties. Poor and fair. 4 pcs.
1134. 1802 and 1803. Varieties. Fair and good. 5 pcs.
1135. 1804. Good for this rare cent. Genuine.
1136. 1805 and 1806. Fair. Scarce. 2 pcs.
1137. 1807 and 1808. Varieties. Fair and good. 3 pcs.
1138. 1809. Very fair. Rare.
1139. 1810. Good.
1140. 1811. Good. Rare.
1141. 1812, 1813, 1814. Very fair. 3 pcs.
1142. 1816, 1817, 15 and 13 stars. 1818, 1819. Fair to fine. 6 pcs.
1143. 1820 to 1829 inclusive. Average good. Varieties. 12 pcs.
1144. 1830 to 1839 inclusive. Average good. Varieties. 14 pcs.
1145. 1840 to 1849 inclusive. Average good. Varieties. 17 pcs.
1146. 1850 to 1856 inclusive. Average fine. Varieties. 11 pcs.
1147. 1857. Small date. Good.
1147a. 1794 to 1856. Rare dates out. 2 pierced. Fine. 1809 electro. Fair.
    54 pcs.
1147b. 1798 to 1882. Rare dates out. Average. Very fair. 71 pcs.
1148. **Small Cents.** 1856, eagle. Very good indeed. Rare.
1149. 1857 to 1864 inclusive. Nickle. Average fine. 8 pcs.
1150. 1864 to 1882 inclusive. Mostly bright. Copper. 19 pcs.
1151. **Two Cent Pieces.** 1864 to 1872 inclusive. Uncirculated. Scarce.
    9 pcs.
1152. 1864, 1865, 1867, 1868, 1871, 1872. Bright. Scarce. 6 pcs.
1153. 1864. Original red. 5 pcs.
1154. 1865. Original red. 5 pcs.
1155. 1867 and 1868. Original red. 5 pcs.
1156. **Three Cent Nickles.** 1879, 1880, 1881. Good and fine. Scarce. 3 pcs.
1157. **Five Cent Nickles.** 1871 and 1875. Proofs. Scarce. 2 pcs.
1158. 1878. Proof. Rare.
1159. 1879. Uncirculated. Scarce.
1160. 1881. Uncirculated. Scarce.

Odds and Ends.

1161. 1859. Pattern half dollar. Copper silvered. Fine.
1162. 1855. Not one cent, but just as good. Very fair. Scarce.
1163. 1833. Liberia cent. Scarce. Good.
1164. 1788. Connecticut cent, struck over a Unity States. Curious and good,
    but pierced.
1165. 1767. Coin struck for Danish-American Colonies. Fair.
1166. War tokens of 1861 to 1864, with busts of Franklin, Jackson, Mc-
    Clellan, and statute of Washington. Good to bright. 8 pcs.
1167. Business cards in brass and copper. Bright. These belong to the set,
    the dies of which were destroyed in a fire at Waterbury, Conn., some
    years back. They are getting scarce, especially in this condition. No
    duplicates. Large cent size. 10 pcs.
1168. A similar lot. Same size. No duplicates. Fine. 10 pcs.
1169. A similar lot. Smaller size. No duplicates. Fine and uncirculated.
    5 pcs.
1170. Spiel marks. Some with Washington's bust. Different sizes. Fine.
    10 pcs.
1171. Lead copies of rare colonials and patterns. Fine. 11 pcs.

1172. Lead copies of rare medals. Fine. 3 pes.
1173. Lead copies of rare ancient Greek and Roman coins. Fine. 10 pcs.
1174. Curious French medals of antique characters. White metal silvered.
    Good and fine. 5 pes.
1175. English half penny tokens. 1 pierced. Good and fine. 10 pes.
1176. Foreign base metal and copper coins. 1 old. Good and fine. 5 pes.
1177. Shooting medal. Tom Thumb, etc. Uncirculated and fine. 3 pcs.
1178. Mixed counterfeits and castings. Good. 6 pcs.
1179. Jetons and patterns, principally English. Good and fine. 9 pcs.
1180. A curious lot of old medals and tokens in lead, brass and copper.
    Good. 5 pes.

Confederate States, Bonds and Money.

1181. $500 bond. March 2, 1863. Pink paper. Coupons attached. Rare.
1182. $1,000 bond. Jan. 1, 1862. White paper. Coupons attached. Rare.
1183. $1,000 bond. March 2, 1863. Grey paper. Coupons attached. Rare.
1184. $1,000 bond. July 1, 1864. Yellowish paper. Coupons attached. Rare.
1185. $1,000 bond. North Carolina. Jan. 1, 1862. Coupons attached. Rare.
1186. $1,000 bond. North Carolina. Jan. 1, 1863. Coupons attached. Rare.
1187. Confederate bills, State and Government. Face, $138. Fine and rare.
    15 pes.
1188. Confederate bills, State and Government. Face, $133. Fine and rare.
    14 pes.
1189. Confederate bills, State and Government. Face, $122. Fine and rare.
    11 pes.
1190. Confederate bills, State and Government. Face, $107. Fine and rare.
    10 pes.
1191. Confederate bills, State and Government. Face, $107. Fine and rare.
    8 pes.
1192. Confederate bills, State and Government. Face, $107. Fine and rare.
    8 pes.
1193. Confederate bills, State and Government. Face, $106. Fine and rare.
    7 pes.
1194. Confederate bills, State and Government. Face, $106. Fine and rare.
    6 pes.
1195. Confederate bills, State and Government. Face, $106. Fine and rare.
    6 pes.
1196. Confederate bills, State and Government. Face, $106. Fine and rare.
    6 pes.
1197. Confederate State and Government bills. Face, $106. Rare. 6 pes.
1198. Confederate bills. Fine. Face, $85. 4 pes.
1199. Confederate bills. Fine. Face, $85. 4 pes.
1200. Confederate bills. Fine. Face, $85. 4 pes.
1201. Confederate bills. Fine. Face, $85. 4 pes.
1202. Confederate bills. Fine. Face, $85. 4 pes.
1203. Confederate bills. Fine. Face, $85. 4 pes.
1204. Confederate bills. 5 dollar values. Fine. 10 pes.
1205. Confederate bills. 5 dollar values. Fine. 10 pes.
1206. Confederate bills. 5 dollar values. Fine. 11 pes.
1207. Confederate bills. 10 dollar values. Fine. 10 pes.
1208. Confederate bills. 10 dollar values. Fine. 10 pes.
1209. Confederate bills. 10 dollar values. Fine. 10 pes.
1210. Confederate bills. 10 dollar values. Fine. 10 pes.
1211. Confederate bills. 10 dollar values. Fine. 10 pes.
1212. Confederate bills. 10 dollar values. Fine. 16 pes.
1213. Confederate bills. 20 dollar values. Fine. 12 pes.
1214. Confederate bills. 20 dollar values. Fine. 15 pes.

War Envelopes. In the following collection of envelopes are many of the rarest of this curious feature of the late unpleasantness. The satirical and bronzed lots are specially noticeable. For the convenience of buyers who may desire a few of these artistic gems, they have been arranged in small lots. There are no duplicates in any lot, and in fact, less than twenty in the whole collection: for while some may seem identical, a little examination will show them to be varieties. All new and clean.

1215. Bronzed. Portraits of Union Generals. 10 pcs.
1216. Bronzed. Camp scenes. 5 pcs.
1217. Bronzed. Scenes in Baltimore. 10 pcs.
1218. Bronzed. Scenes in Baltimore. 6 pcs.
1219. Bronzed. Scenes in Baltimore. 8 pcs.
1220. Bronzed. Scenes in Washington City. 10 pcs.
1221. Bronzed. Scenes in Alexandria, Va. 13 pcs.
1222. Bronzed. Scenes in Virginia. 11 pcs.
1223. Bronzed. Scenes in different sections. 11 pcs.
1224. Bronzed. Scenes of army life. 8 pcs.
1225. Bronzed. Scenes of battles. 12 pcs.
1226. Mixed colors. Portraits. Gen. Scott. 14 pcs.
1227. Mixed colors. Portraits. Gen. Scott. 14 pcs.
1228. Mixed colors. Portraits. Gen. Fremont. 14 pcs.
1229. Mixed colors. Portraits, Gens. Butler, Burnside and Banks. 15 pcs.
1230. Mixed colors. Portrait. Gen. McClellan. 20 pcs.
1231. Mixed colors. Portraits of different Colonels. 15 pcs.
1232. Mixed colors. Portrait. Lincoln. 20 pcs.
1233. Mixed colors. Portraits of different Generals. 23 pcs.
1234. Mixed colors. Portraits of Generals with maps attached. 10 pcs.
1235. Mixed colors. Portrait of Washington. 12 pcs.
1236. Mixed colors. Eagles and shields. 20 pcs.
1237. Mixed colors. Eagles and flags. 21 pcs.
1238. Mixed colors. Eagles and flags. 15 pcs.
1239. Mixed colors. Men and flags. 20 pcs.
1240. Mixed colors. Men and flags. 20 pcs.
1241. Mixed colors. Men and flags. 20 pcs.
1242. Mixed colors. Women and flags. 25 pcs.
1243. Mixed colors. Women and flags. 25 pcs.
1244. Mixed colors. Flags. 18 pcs.
1245. Mixed colors. Flags. 20 pcs.
1246. Mixed colors. Flags. 20 pcs.
1247. Mixed colors. Flags. 20 pcs.
1248. Mixed colors. Flags and mixed designs. 17 pcs.
1249. Mixed colors. Female figures. 18 pcs.
1250. Mixed colors. Female figures. 25 pcs.
1251. Mixed colors. Male figures. 15 pcs.
1252. Mixed colors. Male figures. 16 pcs.
1253. Mixed colors. Contrabands. 14 pcs.
1254. Mixed colors. Contrabands. 15 pcs.
1255. Mixed colors. States. 21 pcs.
1256. Mixed colors. States. 21 pcs.
1257. Mixed colors. Army corps. 17 pcs.
1258. Mixed colors. Army corps. 18 pcs.
1259. Mixed colors. Naval expedition. 9 pcs.
1260. Mixed colors. Battle and camp scenes. 16 pcs.
1261. Mixed colors. Scenes in Washington, Baltimore, etc. 20 pcs.
1262. Mixed colors. Scenes in Virginia. 13 pcs.
1263. Mixed colors. Ellsworth, portraits and scenes. 14 pcs.
1264. Mixed colors. Mixed figures. 17 pcs.

1265. Mixed colors. Mixed designs. 20 pcs.
1266. Mixed colors. Mixed designs. 20 pcs.
1267. Mixed colors. Mixed designs. 20 pcs.
1268. Mixed colors. Mixed views. 19 pcs.
1269. Mixed colors. Mixed views. 20 pcs.
1270. Mixed colors. Secession chain. Portraits of Southern Generals. 13 pcs.
1271. Mixed colors. Northern satirical. 25 pcs.
1272. Mixed colors. Northern satirical. 25 pcs.
1273. Mixed colors. Northern satirical. 25 pcs.
1274. Mixed colors. Northern satirical. 25 pcs.
1275. Mixed colors. Northern satirical. 25 pcs.
1276. Mixed colors. Northern satirical. 25 pcs.
1277. Mixed colors. Northern satirical. 25 pcs.
1278. Mixed colors. Northern satirical. 25 pcs.
1279. Mixed colors. Northern satirical. 25 pcs.
1280. Mixed colors. Northern satirical. 25 pcs.
1281. Mixed colors. Northern satirical. 25 pcs.
1282. Mixed colors. Northern satirical. 25 pcs.
1283. Mixed colors. Northern satirical. 25 pcs.
1284. Mixed colors. Northern satirical. 25 pcs.
1285. Mixed colors. Northern satirical. 25 pcs.

U. S. and Foreign Coins, Medals, etc.

1286. 1876. Twenty Cents. Brilliant proof. Scarce.
1287. 1801. Dime. Very fair. Rare.
1288. 1802. Dime. Date distinct. Rare.
1289. 1822. Dime. Good. Very rare.
1290. 1795, 1800. Half Dimes. Very good, but pierced. 2 pcs.
1291. 1801. Cent. 1-000 & II. var., very good. 1862, 1871 Cents. Proofs. 3 pcs.
1292. 1794. Half Cent. Very good. Scarce.
1293. 1846. Half Cent. Mint restrike. Fine and genuine, but has been in a fire.
1294. 1873. Minor proof set, including the rare 2 cent.
1295. 1877, 1879, 1881. Minor proof sets, first is extra rare. 3 sets.
1296. 1795. Washington Grate Cent. Very fine.
1297. Judaea. Mite of Claudius Felix, procurator year 5 of Nero, very good.
1298. Roman denarii of Antonius, Aurelius, etc.; 1st Br. of Commodus. Fine. 8 pcs.
1299. Church Communicants oval leaden tokens. Perth and Scone parishes. Fine. 2 pcs.
1300. 1716. Olmutz. Crown of Wolfgand V. Very fine. Scarce.
1301. 1665-1795. English Penny, Halfpenny, and Farthing tokens. Fine lot. 16 pcs.
1302. Foreign Coppers, including Guernsey, Caracas, etc. Good lot. 111 pcs.
1303. Cyrus W. Field, for Atlantic Cable. Bronze and w. m. 3 pcs.
1304. Garfield (4). Barnum's White Elephant, two very large white metal medals of James Madison, portrait of Washington in wood from Mt. Vernon, etc. Very choice lot of medals. 17 in copper or bronze, 2 in silver. Nearly all proofs. Desirable lot. 50 pcs.
1305. $500 C. S. A. Bond with coupons attached.
1306. Butler and Kearney Fiat money, C. S. A. notes, etc. 30 pcs.
1307. Badges. Log Cabin. LaFayette, Clay. All different. 10 pcs.
1308. Centennial walnut wood medals, size 40. Independence Hall. Washington and Genl. Hawley. A dozen of each. 36 pcs.
1309. The Coinages of the World, Matthews. 300 pages, paper covers, new.
1310. Japanese book, 54 colored pictures, each 7x9 inches.
1311. Japanese clay figures, mostly 3 inches high. Very odd. 18 pcs.

1312. Magnifying glass of two lenses in case.
1313. Egyptian clay bottle.
1314. Fine specimen of brain coral.
1315. Dancing figure in case.
1316. Fine fossil specimen. Pecopteris Miltoni, carboniferous group.
1317. Indian arrow heads (78), celts (2), stone balls (2). Good lot. 82 pcs.
1318. **Cents.** 1799. Much worn, but the date and head very plain; rev., poor. Rare.
1319. 1794 to 1857. Nearly every date, includes 6 of 1857 and varieties of many. The owner's entire collection, except the 1799. No 1804 or '09. Also, 2 half cents, 4 tokens. 211 pcs.

Miscellaneous Coins, etc.

1320. 1802. Dollar. Much worn. Date good.
1321. 1806 to 1836. Half dollars. Nearly every date. One pierced. Good to fine. 32 pcs.
1322. 1831, 1835, 1838. Quarters. Ordinary. 3 pcs.
1323. 1814 to 1883. Dimes. Varieties in dates and mintages. Poor to uncirculated. 67 pcs.
1324. Half dimes. Varieties in dates. 4 pierced. Good lot. 44 pcs.
1325. Silver three cents. Ordinary. 40 pcs.
1326. Large copper cents. Ordinary. 272 pcs.
1327. Nickel and bronze cents. Good to uncirculated. 225 pcs.
1328. Half cent, foreign coppers, etc. Some pierced. 12 pcs.
1329. Foreign silver, English florin, Canada 50 cts., etc., some pierced. 27 pcs.
1330. American Journal of Numismatics, 1882-1884. 8 Nos.
1331. Numisma. Vol. 1 to Vol. 7 complete. 42 Nos.
1332. Frossard's Monograph of U. S. cents and half cents. Finely bound.
1333. Fine velvet-lined coin trays. 8 pcs.
1334. Priced catalogues, including Crosby, Woodwards 46th and 56th (both with plates), Berg., etc., (9). Also circulars, pamphlets, etc., (16). 25 pcs.
1335. Jewell's works, London, 1669. Large volume, hundreds of pages. Finely bound in calf.
1336. The Spectator, London, 1711. With portrait of Pope. 272 pages.
1337. Garfield gold medalet. Half dollar size. Proof.
1338. Fine photograph of Guiteau, with *autograph*.
1339. 5 and 10 cents. Frac. currency. Broad margin. Separated. 2 pcs.
1340. 245 B. C. Kew-taou, one of the largest of the Taou coins of China. Razor shaped. Has been broken and mended Very fine and rare. 144x19.
1341. Collection of Chinese curiosities, including a very fine portrait in case, brass combs, Joss sticks, paper dollar, porcelain ring, etc. 15 pcs.
1342. Arrow heads. Lanc. Co., Pa., *white quartz*. Good lot. 111 pcs.
1343. Arrow heads. White quartz. Balance of lot. Poor to fair. 134 pcs.
1344. Balance of the Indian collection. Some good arrows, some poorer; also, about 25 or more odds and ends mostly imperfect, including pottery, pieces of pipe stems, a large rude celt, jasper from which arrows have been chipped, broken perforated pendants, parts of a soapstone dish, etc. 280 pcs.
1345. Box containing sandstone noodles with fossil ferns, minerals, etc. Desirable.
1346. Similar box. Equally choice.
1347. Another box as fine as the last two.

U. S. Silver, etc.

1348. 1798 Dollar. Good.
1349. 1795 Half Dollar, fair; 1806, 1809, 1810, etc.; good to uncir. 14 pcs.

1350. 1815 Quarter, fair; 1833, 1837. Dimes of 1857. '59, '76, '82 to '84, last 3 uncir'd. 9 pcs.
1351. Cents, 1798, 1803, 1806, 1807, etc. *No duplicates.* A good lot. 35 pcs.
1352. 1788. Vermont cent. Good.
1353. Minor sets, *uncirculated.* 1863 cent ; 1864, 1, 2 cts ; 1865, 2, 3 cts ; 1866, 1, 2, 3, 5 cts ; 1867, 1, 3 cts ; 1868, 1, 3, 5 cts ; 1869, 1, 3 cts ; 1870, 3, 5 cts ; 1871, 3, 5 cts ; 1872, 3 cts ; 1873, 1, 3, 5 cts ; 1874, 1875, 1876, complete ; 1877, cent (2). 1881 minor proof set ; 1882, 1, 5 cts ; 1883, 1, 5 cts (2) ; 1884, 1, 5 cts. In *uncirculated* condition, generally scarcer than proof. 46 pcs.

Relics of President Buchanan.

The following, purchased at the sale at Wheatland, President Buchanan's home, a few miles from Lancaster, Pa., are the balance of these very interesting remembrances of the late President, a portion being sold in our last sale. A considerable portion are of the period of his career as Minister to England.

1354. *Original draft* of the President's Annual Message to Congress, December, 1859, *in his own handwriting.* This long and interesting message was written just before the exciting events of the late war, and is very desirable.
1355. Letters of invitations to dinners, receptions, etc., while Minister to England, from members of Parliament. Lords, etc. Includes one from Palmerston, "I hope I shall meet your pretty niece." Letter sheets. 33 pcs.
1356. Similar cards of invitations. 50 pcs.
1357. Buchanan's personal cards of invitation. "Mr. Buchanan requests," etc. 43 pcs.
1358. Visiting cards received by Buchanan. Ingersoll. Brewster. McClure, and others are represented. 75 pcs.
1359. Similar lot. Equally desirable. 77 pcs.
1360. Pamphlets, written and printed. Includes Buchanan's Fire Insurance of 1829, programme of Lord Mayor of London's parade, 1854, etc. 19 pcs.

Old Newspapers, Almanacs, etc.

1361. A remarkable collection of early newspapers, including the Maryland Journal, 1773, with advertisement of Gen'l Washington ; Penn'a Gazette, 1773 ; Penn'a Packet, 1775 ; Penn'a Evening Post, 1779 ; New Jersey Gazette, 1779 ; Continental Journal, 1785 (title cut is the reverse of a Washington cent) ; Brunswick Gazette, 1787 ; Connecticut Journal, 1788 ; Vermont Journal, 1789 ; Salem Gazette, 1794 ; Mercantile Advertiser, 1798 ; True American, 1799 ; N. Y. Price Current, 1808. A very fine and desirable lot. 13 pcs.
1362. National Intelligencer, Aug. 19, 1824, announcing the arrival of Gen'l Lafayette. Very fine.
1363. The Log Cabin, 1840. *Horace Greeley and Co.* 8 Nos.
1364. Rebellion papers. Louisiana Signal, 1860 ; Christian Banner, 1862 ; Magnolia Weekly, 1863 ; The Patriot, 1855 ($20 per annum). 4 pcs.
1365. Old almanacs. 1807 to 1849. Fine and very fine. 13 pcs.
1366. Old almanacs. 1785, 1794, 1796, 1799, 1800, 1803, 1807, 1808, etc. Some imperfect, but many good. 40 pcs.
1367. 1865. Chaudron's Confederate Spelling Book. Very fine.
1368. 1836. Farmers' Map of Michigan and Ouisconsin (note spelling). Large size.
1369. $100 note of First National Bank of Boston. Proof impressions of obverse and reverse on cardboard in right colors from original plates.
1370. Chinese Primer. Chinese Book, "Bongobola Prokaseeka," Ningpo Gazette, and four others, all native work ; also, large picture. 9 pcs.
1371. Chinese Almanac, native Canton print, illustrated and printed in three

colors. Several hundred pages, including hundreds of comic pictures. Very odd and desirable.

1372. Japanese school books. One Vol. each on Birds, Beasts, Fishes and Man. Remarkably odd and curious native designs, highly colored. 20 pages each : 4 Vols.

1373. Japanese Picture Book. 10 double page colored native plates, much finer than usual, and of truly artistic design. Unfolds so as to measure 12 feet long. Cost $4.

1374. Japanese Picture Book, equally choice, but smaller, measures nearly 10 feet when unfolded, ornamental cover. Cost $3. This and the last are of a superior class to those usually sold.

1375. Chinese Gambling Checks. Cardboard engraved in various designs. 28 pcs.

1376. Centennial Silk Book Markers. Washington's Head. 7½ and 9¼ in., 2 pcs.

1377. Silk Badges. Harrison, Clay, and Washington. Choice lot. 22 pcs.

1378. 1791. Elizabethtown Lottery Tickets. Very fine. 9 pcs.

1379. Engravings. Washingtons. Several over 50 years old. No duplicates. 50 pcs.

1380. War Envelopes. *Confederate*. No duplicates. 30 pcs.

1381. War Envelopes. Union. Great variety. No duplicates. 100 pcs.

1382. War Envelopes. Union. Great variety. 500 pcs.

1383. *Colonial*. New Hampshire. 1780. Very good. Canceled. 11 pcs.

1384. Massachusetts. 1780. Good to new. Canceled. 30 pcs.

1385. New Jersey. 1757-1776. Poor to fine. 19 pcs.

1386. Penn'a. 1773. Fine lot. 46 pcs.

1387. Penn'a. Another lot. Poor to good. 110 pcs.

Confederate Notes.

N. B.—None of the following notes are canceled.

1388. 1861. July 25. $10. Female leaning on a shield on which is a Confederate flag. Very fine. Rare.

1389. 1861. July 25. $10. Similar, but smaller "10" to left. Very fine.

1390. 1861. July 25. $5. Similar design. Good. *Very rare*.

1391. 1861. Sept. 2. $50. Train of cars in centre. Fine. *Very rare*.

1392. 1861. Sept. 2. $20. 3 females in centre. Very fine. *Very rare*.

1393. 1861. Sept. 2. $20. Stephens in lower left corner. Very fine. 14 pcs.

1394. 1861. Sept. 2. $20. Stephens in centre. XX in green. Extra fine.

1395. 1861. Sept. 2. $20. Ship. Fine and uncir'd. 26 pcs.

1396. 1861. Sept. 2. $10. Females with urn. Very fine. 13 pcs.

1397. 1861. Sept. 2. $10. Group of Indians. Fine. *Very rare*.

1398. 1861. Sept. 2. $5. Group of females in centre, statue of Washington to right. 5's in red. Very fine. *Very rare*.

1399. 1861. Sept. 2. $5. Female seated. Very fine lot. 45 pcs.

1400. 1861 and 1862 issues. Fine lot, none in last lots. 16 pcs.

1401. 1862. $100. Negroes hoeing. Uncirculated. 39 pcs.

1402. 1862. $50. Jeff Davis. New. Rare. 7 pcs.

1403. 1863. Apr. 6 $50 (3), 20 (10), 10 (10), 5. V. fine to new. 24 pcs.

1404. 1864. Feb. 17. $100. *Small note*. Uncirculated. Rare.

1405. 1864. Feb. 17. $20. No series, series 1 to 10, A to D of each. Complete uncirculated set. 44 pcs.

1406. 1864. Feb. 17. $2. Uncirculated. Crisp. 25 pcs.

1407. 1864. Feb. 17. $1 (16), 2 (31). Good to new. 47 pcs.

1408. 1864. Feb. 17. 50 cts. to $500. Very fine set. 9 pcs.

The following State notes are uncanceled, some very rare.

1409. North Carolina. $50 (21). $20 (50), $3 (9), $2 (33), $1 (7), 50 cts. (10), 25 cts. (18). 10 cts. (3). 5 cts. New and crisp. 179 pcs.

1410. Virginia, North Carolina, South Carolina, Georgia, Florida, Alabama, Mississippi, Louisiana. 5 cts to $50. Well mixed, fine lot, many var's. 105 pcs.

1411. Southern State Notes of Va., N. C., Ga., Ala., Miss., Tenn. All different notes—not varieties—and some exceedingly scarce. A fine lot. 44 pcs.
1412. Southern State Notes. Duplicates from the last lot, and in very good condition. A great variety, very well mixed. 135 pcs.
1413. Confederate bonds. $100 (1863), $500 (1864.) Signed. 2 pcs.
1414. N. C. County Bonds (2), C. S. A. $100. Non-taxable Certificates (2), C. S. A. Deposit Certificates (10). Fac-similes of rare C. S. A. Notes (8). Reprints from captured C. S. A. Note plate (4). 26 pcs.

Stamps.

The following 7 lots are known as "India ink proofs," *not* stamped with word "specimen" as usually found.

1415. State Department. 3, 6, 7, 10 cts. 3 of each. 12 pcs.
1416. War Department. Complete set. 1 to 90 cts. 11 pcs.
1417. Navy Department. Complete set. 1 to 90 cts. 11 pcs.
1418. Justice Department. Complete set. 1 to 90 cts. 10 pcs.
1419. Interior Department. Complete set. 1 to 90 cts. 10 pcs.
1420. 1869. U. S. Postage. Complete set. 1 to 90 cts. 10 pcs.
1421. 1879. U. S. Postage Due. Complete set. 1 to 50 cts. 7 pcs.
1422. Stamp Album, Scott's International, cloth cover, contains 315 stamps, including full set of War, Interior, Post-Office, etc. Also portraits of rulers, flags and arms of all nations. Desirable collection.
1423. Another collection, also neatly mounted in a Scott's International Album. Includes 29 U. S. Postage, 40 U. S. Official, including Agriculture, State, Navy, etc.; also, a great variety of Foreign, making a total of 753 different stamps, in addition to 113 Hamburg locals, or 866 altogether. Among the lot are a number of scarce stamps, and it would make a nice nucleus for a very large collection.
1424. Swedish stamps. Well mixed, good for a dealer. About 1200 stamps.
1425. U. S. Postage stamps. 1, 2, 3 cts. Used. 2455 pcs.
1426. U. S. Envelope stamps. 1 ct. (66), 2 cts. (14), 3 cts. (202). 282 pcs.
1427. Shanghai, Japan, Ceylon, etc. Unused Postal Cards. No duplicates. 36 pcs.
1428. U. S. 3 cent stamped envelopes of the earliest issue, entire, rare (4). Boyd's Local and early U. S. stamps on original envelopes. Centennial green 3 ct., new, and other U. S. envelopes entire. 17 pcs.
1429. Foreign Stamped Envelopes, entire, no duplicates. 10 pcs.
1430. British Tax Stamp, 1795, similar to those that caused the Revolution.
1431. Mishler's Herb Bitters, 6 cts., black. A very rare revenue stamp. 10 pcs.
1432. Centennial Stamp Album, spaces for 1460 stamps, new.
1433. Stamp Album, larger than last, cloth, new.
1434. War 1 ct. wrappers (8), P. O. Department 3 and 6 cts. envelopes entire (32). 40 pcs.
1435. American Stamp Mercury, 1867–1870. 12 nos.
1436. American Journal of Philately, Scott & Co., 1873 complete. 12 nos.
1437. Stamp Collector's Magazine, Bath, 1872 ; New Jersey, Ohio, St. Louis, and Michigan Philatelist, Coin and Stamp Journal, and other philatelic papers. 24 nos.
1438. Stamp pamphlets in great variety. 82 pcs.

Curiosities.

1439. Apache bow in buckskin case ; also, quiver with 18 steel-pointed, feather-tipped arrows. Bow 4 feet long. Very choice and desirable.
1440. Chinese Idol. Curiously carved seated wooden figure, lacquered and ornamented. 7 inches in height.
1441. East India Idol. Vishnu seated, high pointed head-dress. Very fine, curious and rare. Bronze. 2¾ inches high.

1442. Chinese Idol. Dog Fo with three tails. Fine bronze. 1½ inches.
1443. Peru. An idol in shape of grotesque human figure. 2 inches.
1444. Curious South Sea Islander's necklace of 43 teeth.
1445. Old Scales, dated 1666. With curious weights of the period. In case.
      Very fine and desirable. Cost $5.
1446. Rebellion relic. Louisiana Tigers. Machete with scabbard. Fine.
1447. Rebellion relic. Dagger made out of a bayonet.
1448. Large Bowie-style knife with spring, fine steel blade, ivory and Ger-
      man silver mounted handle. Length of blade, 9 inches: length of
      handle, 9½ inches. Very formidable weapon, made for the South
      American revolutionary trade.
1449. Florida Sea Beans. Very fine lot. 8 pcs.
1450. Piece of the first Atlantic cable. Brass-bound cabinet specimen.
1451. Collection of fossil teeth of sharks of the Eocene period, from Ashley
      River, S. C., many curious forms neatly arranged on cards, all but 3
      perfect. 35 pcs.
1452. Centennial Liberty Bell pipe. Olive wood. New.
1453. Onyx Marble Slab, chalcedony color, with clouds of red and yellow
      disseminated throughout. Very fine. Would make a choice paper
      weight. 6x2½ inches.
1454. Paintings on ivory. One on copper. Choice. From Perugino. 7 pcs.
1455. Gems, Cleopatra, Dog's head, etc. Small. 4 pcs.
1456. Male head, Greek combat, female and lion, casts, silver (2), iron (1).
      3 pcs.
1457. Paper weights of marble from the "Appian Way." Ravenna, Italy.
      2 pcs.
1458. Cowries. Shells used in Africa as money. 20 pcs.
1459. A suit of clothes worn by Gen'l Tom Thumb, the dwarf.
1460. Japanese jackstraw box, native and curious.
1461. Centennial curiosities, paper-weights, pins, sleeve buttons, brooches,
      miniature 56 lb. weight, etc., mostly with Liberty Bell or views of
      the buildings. Cost at Exhibition, 25 cts. to $1 each. 63 pcs.
1462. Chinese colored native pictures on paper, each 7x11 in. Fine. 12 pcs.

Miscellaneous Coins, etc.

1463. U. S. cents. None pierced but nearly all considerably worn. Some
      early dates. 600 pcs.
1464. Ships, Colonies and Commerce. Partly bright. 55 pcs.
1465. Pins, badges, etc. Centennial, Masonic, etc. Fine lot. 45 pcs.
1466. Phila. Sheep and Wool show medals. Brass proof. Very pretty. 22 pcs.
1467. Set of Centennial wooden medals. Round. In case. 6 pcs.
1468. Set of Centennial wooden medals. Oblong. 2⅜x4 in. 5 pcs.
1469. Hard Times Tokens. Includes Loco Foco, Am I not a woman and
      sister? Feuchtwanger cent, etc. Also a pierced Hog Token in brass.
      No duplicates. Good to very fine. 50 pcs.
1470. Hard Times Tokens. Well mixed lot. Equally good. 50 pcs.
1471. War cards and tokens. *No duplicates.* Fine. 220 pcs.
1472. War cards and tokens. *No duplicates.* Good to uncirculated. 120 pcs.
1473. War cards and tokens. *No duplicates.* Very good. 105 pcs.
1474. War cards and tokens. *No duplicates.* Very good. 75 pcs.
1475. War cards and tokens. Very good. Great variety. 500 pcs.
1476. Base silver, Turkey, (dollar size), Hungary, Danish America, etc.
      Average about 25 cent size. Fair to very good. *All different.* 20 pcs.
1477. Base silver. Hamburg, Oldenburg, Wurtemberg, Frankfort, Hesse,
      Danish America, Turkey, etc. Average about dime size. Fair to very
      fine. *All different.* 56 pcs.
1478. Stonewall Jackson medals. Tin proof (size 32) in lacquered frame.
      15 pcs.

1479. Stonewall Jackson medals. Similar medals in morocco case. 6 pcs.
1480. Store cards, size of old copper cent. Very fine to proof. A very desirable lot. *No duplicates.* 48 pcs.
1481. Tobacco and temperance medals, store cards, California counters, political and hard times tokens. Average very good. 31 pierced. 68 pcs.
1482. Omnibus, ferry and bridge tokens. 4 pierced. Rare lot. 9 pcs.
1483. Store cards, size of copper cent. Uncirculated. Brilliant. *No duplicates.* 63 pcs.
1484. Large store cards, medalets, etc. Uncirculated. Brilliant. *No duplicates.* 35 pcs.
1485. Large store cards. Good to uncirculated. *No duplicates.* 85 pcs.
1486. Large store cards. Fair to fine. *No duplicates.* 40 pcs.
1487. Cards, tokens, etc. Fair to fine. *No duplicates.* 93 pcs.

Ancient Coins.

1488. Roman Great Bronze. Poor to good, mostly about fair. Includes many of the Emperors, from the Cæsars to John Zimiscés (Bust of Christ.) 45 pcs.
1489. Roman Great and Middle Bronze. Mostly very poor. 50 pcs.
1490. Roman Great and Middle Bronze. Another lot, equal to last. 100 pcs.
1491. Roman Middle Bronze. Fair to good. Includes one with heads of Julius and Augustus Cæsar; also, others of Augustus, Tiberius, Claudius, Vespasian, Domitian, Trajan, etc. 31 pcs.
1492. Roman Third Bronze. Era of Constantine. Very good to very fine. *All different.* 25 pcs.
1493. Roman Third Bronze. Good lot. 50 pcs.
1494. Roman Third Bronze. Equally good lot. 72 pcs.
1495. Roman Third Bronze. Very poor lot. 127 pcs.
1496. Roman Third Bronze. Poor to fair. 55 pcs.
1497. Roman Family and Imperial Denarii. Mostly ancient counterfeits. Fair. 20 pcs.
1498. Greek Bronze of various sizes. Poor to very good. A very fair lot with some scarce pieces, including Sicily, Rhodes, etc. 38 pcs.
1499. Ancient Bactria. Heremus Soter. B. C. 120. Bust to right; rev., Hercules. Fair to good. 14 pcs.

Foreign Coppers.

1500. Bavaria (24). Bamberg (5). Very good lot, two dated 1622. 29 pcs.
1501. Belgium. 1, 2, 5, 10 Cent. Very good. 72 pcs.
1502. Central America. Mountain peaks. About fair, or as usually found. 33 pcs.
1503. China. Cash. Nice clean specimens. 100 pcs.
1504. China. Cash. Similar lot. 500 pcs.
1505. England. Halfpenny Tokens. Poor to fine. 8 pierced. 53 pcs.
1506. German States. Great variety. No duplicates. Fair to fine. 212 pcs.
1507. German States. A great variety. *No duplicates.* Fair to fine. 155 pcs.
1508. Germany. 1, 2, 3 Pfennig. Good lot. 144 pcs.
1509. Germany. Good and very good. 461 pcs.
1510. India, Turkey, and Egypt. Good lot, including Island of Sumatra, etc. No duplicates. 70 pcs.
1511. Japan. Tempos. Very good. 100 pcs.
1512. Japan. Tempos. Equally good lot. 500 pcs.
1513. Japan. Rins. Uncirculated, a number bright red. 100 pcs.
1514. Jettons, etc. Good lot. 86 pcs.
1515. Mecklenburg. Fine lot. 17 pcs.
1516. Morocco. ¼, ½, 1 Flu. Fair to good. 17 pcs.
1517. Munster. Good lot. 44 pcs.
1518. Oldenburg. Good lot. 83 pcs.

1519. Poland. 3 Groszy, etc. Very good. 94 pcs.
1520. Rostock. Griffan. Good lot. 79 pcs.
1521. Russia. Large 5 kopecs, weight 2 oz. Very good. 5 pcs.
1522. Schleswick-Holstein. Good lot. 124 pcs.
1523. Siam. Pewter cash. 200 pcs.
1524. Siam. Pewter cash. 500 pcs.
1525. Sinaloa. ¼ Real. Good and rare lot. 24 pcs.
1526. Spain. Great variety, some very early. A desirable, good lot. 125 pcs.
1527. Spiel Markes, some with head of Washington. Very good. 50 pcs.
1528. Sweden, Norway and Denmark. Good lot. No duplicates. 25 pcs.
1529. Sweden. Coppers in great variety. Some very scarce. A very good lot. 100 pcs.
1530. Sweden. Baron Goertz Dalers. Mercury, Mars, etc. Fair to very good. 15 pcs.
1531. Turkey. Variety, two octagonal, some rare. Very good. 19 pcs.
1532. Turkey. A very good lot. 50 pcs.
1533. Turkey. Copper cent size and larger. Very good. 92 pcs.
1534. Uruguay, Poland, Spain, etc. A good lot. *No duplicates.* 200 pcs.
1535. Uncirculated, beautiful bright red coppers of Canada, Saxe-Meiningen, Reuss, Russia, India, France, Greece, Hong Kong, etc. 127 pcs.
1536. Coppers of penny size and larger. Barely fair to very fine. *No duplicates.* 75 pcs.
1537. Coppers. Selections from many lands and all sizes. Fair to uncirculated. *No duplicates.* 500 pcs.
1538. Coppers. *No duplicates.* Very fair lot. 260 pcs.
1539. Coppers. *No duplicates.* Barely fair to very fine. 126 pcs.
1540. Coppers. *No duplicates.* Poor to fine. 160 pcs.
1541. Coppers. Mostly poor, but unpierced. 300 pcs.
1542. Coppers. Mostly poor or very poor, about ½ pierced. 304 pcs.
1543. Coppers. Mostly poor. Unpierced. 350 pcs.
1544. Coppers. Pierced, mostly U. S. Cents. 142 pcs.

The following lots of coppers are in all conditions, except very poor or pierced, those in that condition having been taken out. They will average good or even better, and some rare pieces will probably be found among them.

1545. Miscellaneous Foreign Coppers. 100 pcs.
1546. Miscellaneous Foreign Coppers. 200 pcs.
1547. Miscellaneous Foreign Coppers. 500 pcs.
1548. Miscellaneous Foreign Coppers. 1000 pcs.

Coin Books, etc.

1549. Dickeson's American Numismatic Manual. 19 fine plates, colored to represent the metal of the coins. Large 4to. Cloth. Out of print.
1550. "Early Coins of America," by S. S. Crosby. Boston, 1875. The standard and exhaustive work on the subject. Finely bound. Cost $12 unbound.
1551. Same as last, but in parts as issued, with all the plates.
1552. The Coin Book. Lippincott & Co., 1878. Printed on fine, heavy paper, and illustrated with 32 plates of U. S. and Foreign coins. Cloth. New. 140 pages.
1553. Bolen's Medals, by Johnson, cloth, intervened.
1554. Haseltine's Type Table Catalogue. Paper covers.
1555. An Arrangement of Copper Cents, 1816–57, Andrews, pamphlet.
1556. Humphrey's Coin Collector's Manual. Many plates. An excellent work on Ancient and British coins. 2 vols.
1557. The Coin Collector's Manual. Geo. T. Jones. 1860. 4to. Cloth.
1558. Current Gold and Silver Coins of all nations. Ivan C. Michels, 1880. Cloth. 112 pages. Hundreds of illustrations.
1559. Varieties of the Copper issues of U. S. Mint in 1794. Dr. Maris.

1560. Tables of the value of gold and silver, Boston. 1756. Early pamphlet.
1561. Records of Roman History, from Pompeius to Tiberius Constantinus, as exhibited on coins. 2 vol's. 4to. Cloth. London. 1860. Valuable and interesting.
1562. An account of English money, etc., Bishop Fleetwood. London. 1745. 180 pages. 12 plates of coins. Calf, one cover loose. Rare.
1563. Tallis' History and Description of the Crystal Palace Exhibition. London. 1851. 6 volumes issued at a cost of over $15. Hundreds of beautiful steel engravings illustrating the beauties of this exhibition.
1564. Illustrated Encyclopedia of Animated Nature. 384 pages: 1350 illustrations. Fine and desirable.
1565. Coinages of the World. Matthews. 1876. Cloth, new, many illustrations. 306 pages.
1566. Same as last, but in paper covers.
1567. Robinson Crusoe's Money. Illustrated by Nast. 8 vo., cloth. 118 pages. New.
1568. Catalogue of the Bushnell sale. 6 days, hand priced, rare.
1569. Cloth Album for Confederate Currency, C. H. Bechtel. 1871. The only album of its class, and just what is needed. New.

Fractional Currency.

(All new and clean, unless otherwise stated.)

1570. 50, 25, 10, 5 cts. First issue. Perforated edges. 4 pcs.
1571. 50 cts. Justice seated. Red back. Autographic signatures.
1572. 50 cts. Justice seated. Green back.
1573. 50 cts. Spinner. Red back. Autographic signatures.
1574. 50 cts. Spinner. Red back.
1575. 50 cts. Spinner. Green back. "50" in centre and "50" at ends. 2 pcs.
1576. 25 cts. Fessenden. Printed on coarse, heavy, greyish-white paper with numerous fibres, has on the back in gilt, M-2-6-5. Very rare.
1577. 15 cts. Red and green backs. Grant and Sherman. Rare. 2 pcs.
1578. 15 cts. Same. Red and green backs. Circulated. Front and back pasted together. Rare. 2 pcs.
1579. 10 cts. Washington. Red back.
1580. 5 cts. Clark. Red back.
1581. 50 cts., Lincoln and Stanton; 25 cts., Washington: 15, 10 cts., Liberty. Fourth issue complete. 4 pcs.
1582. 50 cts., Crawford and Dexter: 25 cts., Walker: 10 cts., Meredith, red and green seals. Fifth issue complete. 5 pcs.

The following are each in two pieces, front and back separate, mostly stamped on the blank reverse with SPECIMEN in gilt :

1583. 50 cts. Justice seated. Autographic and lithographic signatures together with one green back. Sold as 3 notes.
1584. 50 cts. Justice seated. Auto. sign. of Colby and Spinner, gr. back.
1585. 50 cts. Spinner. Red back (autographic) and green back. 2 pcs.
1586. 25 cts. Fessenden. Red back. Front pasted on card-board.
1587. 10 cts. Washington. Red back (auto. and lithographic) and green back. 3 pcs.
1588. 5 cts. Clark. Red and green back. 2 pcs.
1589. 3 cts. Washington. 4 pcs.

Autographs.

1590. **Geo. Washington.** Feb. 4, 1789. Letter to John Sullivan signed by the father of our country in his well-known round hand. In splendid condition.
1591. Geo. Washington. Dec. 5, 1782. From headquarters, Newburgh, N. Y. "For some time past I have been fully pursuaded that the British had been tampering with some individuals within our lines," etc. In-

teresting war letter, signed by Washington. Has been much folded, and the paper is weak in consequence; but the writing is plain, and signature excellent.

1592. Thos Jefferson. June 22, 1808. Autograph letter in the third person franked on outside with autograph signature. Very fine.

1593. James Madison. June 23, 1808. Splendid autograph letter in best possible condition.

1594. Mrs. Madison. Initials D. P. M. to autograph letter. Franked in autograph by *James Madison*, and therefore containing autographs of both the President and his wife.

1595. James Buchanan. Sept. 7, 1858. Splendid autograph letter to the officers of the African Colonization Society in reply to an offer of $45,000 to the U. S. for the 300 negroes at Fort Sumpter and their maintenance in Africa for one year.

1596. Thaddeus Stevens. "The Great Commoner." Very fine autograph letter.

1597. Dr. Witt Clinton. Jan. 23, 1812. Very fine autograph letter. Marked "confidential."

1598. David Porter, Gov. of Penn'a. 1841. Autograph note. Very fine.

1599. F. R. Shunk, Gov. of Penn'a. Very long and interesting autograph letter on the financial affairs of the State "to his old school-mate. James Buchanan."

1600. Jared Sparkes. Autograph letter to Buchanan. 1842.

1601. N. Biddle, Philadelphia. Autograph letter to Buchanan. 1833.

Confederate Notes.

Among the following will be found some extremely desirable specimens. *Those described as canceled by clean cuts have nothing missing from the notes*, the cuts being scarcely visible, except on close inspection. They are not those usually sold with the semi-circles cut from bottom.

1602. 1861. $1000. Montgomery issue. National Bank Note Co. Very good. Canceled by two clean cuts. *Exceedingly rare*.

1603. 1861. $100. Richmond. Train of cars running to left. Uncirculated. *Extremely rare*.

1604. 1861. $50. Montgomery. Negroes hoeing in cotton field. Fine. *Very rare*.

1605. 1861. $50. Richmond. Two females seated on a cotton bale. Very good. Canceled by small punch holes. *Very rare*.

1606. 1861. July 25. $5. Richmond. Printed by J. Mauronvier. "Five" on the left end. Rev.. "Confederate States of America" in blue. Very good. *Excessively rare*.

1607. 1861. July 25. $10. Female leaning on a shield on which is a Confederate flag. Fine. Canceled by clean cuts. Rare.

1608. 1861. July 25. $10. Same as last, but smaller "10" to left. Very good. Rare.

1609. 1861. Sept. 2. $50. Train of cars in centre. Very fine. Canceled by clean cuts. *Very rare*.

1610. 1861. Sept. 2. $50. Train of cars. Fine. Canceled. *Very rare*.

1611. 1861. Sept. 2. $20. Stephens in centre. XX in green. V. fine. Rare.

1612. 1861. Sept. 2. $20. Same as last. Very fine. Rare.

1613. 1861. Sept. 2. $20. 3 females in centre. Very fine. *Very rare*.

1614. 1861. Sept. 2. $20. 3 females in centre. Very fine. Canceled by clean cuts. *Very rare*.

1615. 1861. Sept. 2. $20. Kneeling female, globe, etc. Very fine. Canceled by clean cuts. *Very rare*.

1616. 1861. Sept. 2. $20. Kneeling female, globe, etc. Fine. Canceled by clean cuts. *Very rare*.

1617. 1861. Sept. 2. $10. Group of Indians. Extra fine. *Very rare*.

1618. 1861. Sept. 2. $10. Group of Indians. Fine. Canceled by clean cuts. *Very rare.*

1619. 1861. Sept. 2. $10. Wagon loaded with cotton bales. Very fine. Canceled by clean cuts. *Extremely rare*, though not usually so given.

1620. 1861. Sept. 2. $10. Heads of Hunter and Memminger. X's in red. Very fine. 2 pcs.

1621. 1861. Sept. 2. $10. Seated female leaning on a shield. Fine. Canceled with clean cuts. *Very rare.*

1622. 1861. Sept. 2. $5. Machinist and hammer. Very good. Canceled with clean cuts. *Very rare.*

1623. 1861. Sept. 2. $5. Same as last, in same condition. *Very rare.*

1624. 1863. Apr. 6. $100. Head of Mrs. Davis. Uncir'd. 3 pcs.

U. S. Cents, Minor Proof Sets, etc.

1625. **Cents.** 1793. Wreath. Very fine and strong. Handsome clean brown color. Very desirable.

1626. 1793. Chain. Good and rare.

1627. 1794. Separated date. Maris No. 16. Very good.

1628. 1795. Thin planchet. Good.

1629. 1796. Liberty cap. Very good.

1630. 1797. Very good. Bold milling on obverse, better than usual.

1631. 1798. Large date. 1800. Very good. 2 pcs.

1632. 1799. Poor and slightly scratched at date, but, I think, genuine.

1633. 1801. Two curious breaks in die connect the chin with the neck, giving appearance of a beard. Nearly fine. Brown.

1634. 1802, 1803. Fine and of good color. 2 pcs.

1635. 1804. Very good and bold. Rare.

1636. 1805. Very good or fine. Light brown.

1637. 1806. Fine. Strong impression of brown color. Rare so good.

1638. 1807, 1808. Both very good and bold. 2 pcs.

1639. 1809. Good for date. Rare.

1640. 1810, 1812, 1814. Very good and fine. 3 pcs.

1641. 1811. Very good. Slight corrosion on reverse.

1642. 1813. Very fine. Handsome brown color. One of the best I have seen.

1643. 1816. Uncirculated. Bright red.

1644. 1817, 1818. Uncirculated, bright. 2 pcs.

1645. 1819. Nearly uncirculated. Handsome olive.

1646. 1820. Uncirculated. Brilliant red.

1647. 1821, 1822, 1823, 1824, 1825, 1826. Very good, mostly bold. 6 pcs.

1648. 1827. Fine, and of a choice light olive.

1649. 1828 to 1832, 1835 to 1837. Very good or nearly fine, mostly bold. 8 pcs.

1650. 1833. Fine. Light olive.

1651. 1834. Very fine. Choice brown.

1652. 1838. Very fine. Light olive.

1653. 1839. Silly Head. Fine. Light olive.

1654. 1840. Uncirculated. Bright red.

1655. 1841. Very fine. Brown.

1656. 1842. Large date. Very fine. Brown.

1657. 1843. Uncirculated. Olive.

1658. 1844 to 1849. 1847 bright red, 1846 olive. Choice lot. 6 pcs.

1659. 1850 to 1857. Varieties of '50, '51, '56. Uncirculated ex. '54 and '57. Excepting a few pieces, in bright red condition. 12 pcs.

1660. *Proof sets.* 1873. Old style. Dollar, half and dime, tarnished. 10 pcs.

1661. 1884. Proof set. Complete. 7 pcs.

1662. 1864. Minor proof set. Both cents. 3 pcs.

1663. 1865. Minor proof set. 1, 3, 5 cts. 3 pcs.

1664. 1866. Minor proof set. 1, 2, 3, 5 cts. 4 pcs.
1665. 1867. Minor proof set. 4 pcs.
1666. 1868. Minor proof set. 4 pcs. Rare.
1667. 1869. Minor proof set. 4 pcs.
1668. 1870. Minor proof set. 4 pcs.
1669. 1871. Minor proof set. 4 pcs.
1670. 1872. Minor proof set. 4 pcs. Scarce.
1671. 1873. Minor proof set. 4 pcs. Rare.
1672. 1875, 1876. Minor proof set. 3 pcs. 2 sets.
1673. 1877. Minor proof set. 3 pcs. Very rare.
1674. 1878 to 1883. Minor proof sets. 6 sets.
1675. **Half Dimes.** 1829, '33, '37, '38, '40, '56 to '62, & '70. Uncir'd. mint lustre. 13 pcs.
1676. 1863 to 1872 ex. '65, '70. Proof. 8 pcs.
1677. Balance including 1853, no arrows. Good to uncir'd. 15 pcs.
1678. **Three Cents.** 1851. O. mint. 1856, '59. '60. Fine to uncir'd. 4 pcs.

Foreign Coppers, etc.

Among the following will be found many very desirable specimens. *Lots 1680 to 1712 contain no duplicates.*

1679. War cards and tokens. Good. 120 pcs.
1680. Large cards, etc. Good to uncirculated. 50 pcs.
1681. Medalets. Presidential, Centennial, etc. Good to uncir'd. 22 pcs.
1682. Fulton Institute Medal. Lancaster Pa. Uncirculated. Size 33.
1683. Sarawak cent. J. Brooke, and half cent. C. Brooke, fine. 2 pcs.
1684. Sultana. Sumatra. Philippine Islands, St. Helena, Liberia, etc. Fair to fine. 14 pcs.
1685. Half penny tokens, 1794, etc. Very good lot. 28 pcs.
1686. Italy. Good lot. 32 pcs.
1687. South America and Hayti. Good. 30 pcs.
1688. Sweden and Denmark. Good. 44 pcs.
1689. Russia. Mostly large. Some scarce. Good. 20 pcs.
1690. India, Turkey, Persia, etc. Very good. 44 pcs.
1691. German States. Very good. 160 pcs.
1692. Oldenburg, Reuss, Rostock, etc. Good lot. 100 pcs.
1693. Mainz, Munster, Elberfeld, etc. Mostly odd and scarce. 90 pcs.
1694. Russia. Italy, etc. Extra size. Good. 44 pcs.
1695. Monaco, fair; Maderia, good. 2 pcs.
1696. Guernsey (1), Jersey (1). Fine. 8 pcs.
1697. Canadian tokens. Good. 36 pcs.
1698. India, Turkey, etc. Good. 36 pcs.
1699. Foreign coppers. Uncirculated. Bright. 42 pcs.
1700. Foreign coppers. Good lot. 300 pcs.
1701. Foreign coppers. Fair to fine. 180 pcs.
1702. Foreign coppers. Poor to fine. 200 pcs.
1703. Foreign coppers. Very good. 160 pcs.
1704. Foreign coppers. Good. 65 pcs.
1705. **Silver.** Spain, Mexico, Austria, etc. Average 25 cent size. Fair to uncirculated. 17 pcs.
1706. Chili, Costa Rica, Uruguay, etc. Dime size and larger. Fair to uncirculated. 12 pcs.
1707. Europe, Asia and S. America. Dime to 15 cent size. Fine. 2 pierced. 22 pcs.
1708. 3 to 6 cent size. Very good. 2 pierced. 28 pcs.
1709. Edward I. and II. of England. Silver pennies. Bairly fair to good. 6 pcs.
1710. Denmark (10). Danish America. 1701-1831. Sizes 14 to 17. Good. 13 pcs.

1711. Small silver and base. *Uncirculated.* 28 pcs.

The following contain duplicates, and were purchased at the recent large sale of a European collection at Cologne:

1712. Foreign coppers. Good. 330 pcs.
1713. Foreign coppers. Poor to fine. 104 pcs.
1714. Miscellaneous coppers. Poor to good. 230 pcs.
1715. War tokens, etc. Good. 120 pcs.
1716. Russia. 5 Kopecs. 1784–1805. Fine. 6 pcs.
1717. Russia. 1727–1879. Good lot. 32 pcs.
1718. Very large coppers of Russia, Sicily, etc. Good, several scarce. 20 pcs.
1719. Greece. 1828–1870. 4 of Capo d'Istria. Good. 14 pcs.
1720. Hungary (8), Roumania (1), Finland (4). Good to fine. 13 pcs.
1721. Aachen (Aix-la-Chapelle). 1737–92. B. fair to very good. 21 pcs.
1722. Greitz, 1761–1832 (14), Hesse (26). Barely fair to very good. 40 pcs.
1723. Saxony. Few, if any, duplicates. Good lot. 43 pcs.
1724. Saxe-Weimar, Meiningen, Coburg, Altenburg, etc. Good. Few, if any, duplicates. 40 pcs.
1725. Osnabrück (10), Goslar (8). Very good and scarce. 18 pcs.
1726. Ulm, Ilmenau, Eisenberg, Rheda, etc. Good. Rare lot. 28 pcs.
1727. Bremen, 1719–1841 (10), Frankfurt (4 Jews pennies). Good. 16 pcs.
1728. Bavaria, Mecklenberg, Reuss, Schwartzburg, etc. Good. 76 pcs.
1729. Small Mediæval Bracteates. Dilapidated. 200 pcs.
1730. Better lot of Bracteates. 100 pcs.
1731. Another lot of Bracteates. 100 pcs.
1732. Another lot of Bracteates. 50 pcs.
1733. **Ancient Roman.** Augustus and Tiberius. M. B. Poor to fair. 18 pcs.
1734. Claudius, Caligula, etc., to Hadrian. M. B. Poor to fair. 14 pcs.
1735. Trajan (1) and Hadrian. G. B. 3 Greek. Fair. 8 pcs.
1736. Antonius Pius, M. Aurelius, and their wives. G. B. Poor to fair. 9 pcs.
1737. Same, but Middle Bronze. Barely fair. 9 pcs.
1738. Commodus (4), S. Severus (2), Maximus (1). G. B. Fair. 7 pcs.
1739. Great and Middle Bronze. Poor. 82 pcs.
1740. Small Bronze. Poor. 110 pcs.
1741. Base or bogus Denarii. 14 pcs.
1742. Gallienus (16), Victorinus (16). S. B. Fair. 32 pcs.

The following lots present a great variety of types, there being seldom two exactly alike. They range in condition from barely fair to nearly fine.

1743. Rude small coins of the 30 Tyrants. Seldom found better. 25 pcs.
1744. Similar. Queer lot. 162 pcs.
1745. Tetricus, Sr. A. D. 267–273. Very good. Both sides plain. 27 pcs.
1746. Tetricus, Sr. Portraits fine. 44 pcs.
1747. Tetricus, Sr. Reverses very good. 35 pcs.
1748. Tetricus, Sr. Fair ordinary lot, of the smoother type, struck in the earlier part of his reign. 84 pcs.
1749. Tetricus, Sr. Struck during his troubles. Odd lot. Nearly as good as they ever were. 152 pcs.
1750. Tetricus, Sr. Inferior but not despicable lot. 265 pcs.
1751. Tetricus, Jr. Heads very good. 25 pcs.
1752. Tetricus, Jr. Fair lot. 86 pcs.
1753. Claudius Gothicus. A. D. 268–270. 35 pcs.
1754. Claudius Gothicus. Struck after his death. "Divo Claudio" Altar 44 pcs.
1755. Claudius Gothicus. Similar to last. Eagle. 19 pcs.
1756. Constantine. Poor to good. 30 pcs.
1757. Constantine's wife and mother. Fair. 7 pcs.
1758. Urbs Roma. Wolf and twins. Poor to good. 11 pcs.
1759. Constantinopolis. Poor to good. 11 pcs.

1760. Constans and Constantius. Poor to good. 100 pcs.
1761. Magnentius. A. D. 350-353. Fair to good. 8 pcs.
1762. Valentian. A. D. 364-375. Fair to good. 25 pcs.
1763. Valens. A. D. 364-378. Fair to good. 44 pcs.
1764. Gratian. A. D. 375-389. Fair to good. 23 pcs.
1765. Duplicates of last 3 lots. Barely fair. 40 pcs.
1766. Honorius and Arcadius. Poor to good. 8 pcs.

United States Proof Sets.

1767. 1868. Splendid proof set. Very scarce. 10 pcs.
1768. 1869. Splendid proof set. 10 pcs.
1769. 1870. Splendid proof set. 10 pcs.
1770. 1872. Splendid proof set. 10 pcs.
1771. 1873. Splendid proof set. Old style. 10 pcs.
1772. 1873. Trade proof set. Arrows at date. 7 pcs.
1773. 1874. Splendid proof set. 7 pcs.
1774. 1875. Splendid proof set. Contains the 20 cent piece. 8 pcs.
1775. 1876. Splendid proof set. Contains the 20 cent piece. 8 pcs.
1776. 1877. Splendid proof set. Contains the 20 cent piece. 8 pcs.
1777. 1878. Trade proof set. Contains the 20 cent piece. 8 pcs.
1778. 1879. Splendid proof set. Both dollars. 8 pcs.
1779. 1880. Splendid proof set. Both dollars. 8 pcs.
1780. 1881. Splendid proof set. Both dollars. 8 pcs.
1781. 1882. Splendid proof set. Both dollars. 8 pcs.
1782. 1883. Splendid proof set. Both dollars. 10 pcs.
1783. 1884. Splendid proof set. (No Trade Dollar this year.) 7 pcs.

United States Gold.

1784. Eagles. 1797. Very fine. Scarce.
1785. 1801. Uncirculated. Scarce.
1786. 1803. Very fine. Scarce.
1787. Half Eagles. 1798. Very fine. Rare.
1788. 1802 over '01, 1803 over '02. Very fine. 2 pcs.
1789. 1804. Beautiful impression. Scarcely circulated. Very scarce.
1790. 1806. Pointed 6. Very fine.
1791. 1806. Knobbed 6. Barely circulated.
1792. 1807. Head to left. Very fine.
1793. 1812. Beautiful impression. Proof surface.
1794. 1861. Pike's Peak. $5. Head of Liberty. Fine.
1795. 1849. Mormon. $2½. "Holiness to the Lord." All-seeing eye. Bishop's cap above. Very good and rare.

United States Silver.

1796. Dollars. 1798. *Fifteen stars. Small eagle.* Handsome bold impression, the hair but little worn. A choice specimen of this rare variety.
1797. 1798. *Thirteen stars. Small eagle.* Fine specimen of this variety.
1798. 1799. Five stars facing. Fine and bold impression. Sharp stars, and shows but little wear. Rare.
1799. 1799. Uncirculated. Mint lustre.
1800. 1800. Bold handsome impression. Uncirculated. Mint lustre.
1801. 1836. *Brilliant proof.* Rare.
1802. 1852. A small hole above the head of Liberty has been skillfully plugged, otherwise the piece is in good condition and the date bold. *Extremely rare.*
1803. 1857. *Proof.* Stars, as usual, not sharp. Rare so fine.
1804. 1858. *Brilliant proof.* Very rare.
1805. 1873, 1875, 1876. Trade dollars. Uncir'd. Mint lustre. Rarer than proof. 3 pcs.

1806. **Half Dollars.** 1820. Small wide date. *Proof.* Slightly rubbed in field. Handsome and sharp.
1807. 1827. Proof impression. Very handsome.
1808. 1829. *Proof.* Brilliant. Handsome and choice.
1809. 1840. Proof impression. Scarce so fine.
1810. **Quarters.** 1796. Fine and strong. Rare.
1811. 1804. Very good. Rare.
1812. 1806. Very fine. Some lustre.
1813. 1815. Uncirculated. Small E above head. Handsome mint lustre.
1814. 1818. Uncirculated. Handsome mint lustre.
1815. 1821. Uncirculated. Sharp and beautiful.
1816. 1822. Exceedingly fine. Traces of lustre. In this condition a very rare coin. Cost $5.
1817. 1825. Uncirculated. Beautiful mint lustre.
1818. 1828. Uncirculated. Sharp and handsome.
1819. 1853. *Without arrows.* Very good and rare.
1820. **Twenty Cents.** 1878. Brilliant proof. Very rare.
1821. **Dimes.** 1827. *Proof.* A choice and handsome piece.
1822. 1829. *Proof impression.* Choice and desirable.
1823. 1831. *Proof.* Choice and handsome.
1824. 1835. *Proof.* Handsome.
1825. 1837. *No stars. Proof.*
1826. 1852. *Splendid proof.* Very rare so fine. Cost $3.50.
1827. 1856. *Splendid proof.* Very rare so fine. Cost $4.
1828. **Half Dimes.** 1794. Very fine, bold and sharp. The hair and eagle's breast barely touched. Cost $10.
1829. 1795. Extremely fine and sharp.
1830. 1796. Very fine and strong. Rare. Cost $8.
1831. 1797. 16 stars. Very fine and bold. Cost $7.60.
1832. 1797. 15 stars. 'Good and rare.
1833. 1800. Hair barely touched. Sharp and handsome. A gem.
1834. 1829. *Proof.* Rare so fine.
1835. 1837. *No stars. Proof.*
1836. 1845. *Uncirculated. Mint bloom.* Rare so fine.
1837. 1852. *Splendid proof.* Very rare.
1838. **Silver Three Cents.** 1851. P. and O. Mints. 1852. 1853. Uncir'd, mint bloom. 4 pcs.
1839. 1854. Uncirculated. Brilliant mint bloom. Very rare so fine.
1840. 1855. Uncirculated. Brilliant mint bloom. Very rare so fine.

United States Cents.

1841. 1793. Wreath. Lettered edge. Good for date. Rare.
1842. 1793. Chain. Very fair. Good for this variety. Rare.
1843. 1794. Scarred head. Maris No. 12. Very good. Nearly fine.
1844. 1794. Fallen 4. Maris No. 20. Very good.
1845. 1794. Short bust. Maris No. 21. Very fine. Glossy light brown.
1846. 1794. Short bust. Maris No. 22. Very good. Brown.
1847. 1794. Large planchet. Maris No. 28. Fine. Steel color.
1848. 1794. Shielded hair. Maris No. 32. Fine. Chocolate color.
1849. 1797. A magnificent cent of brilliant original red color and by far the strongest impression of this date I have ever met with. Obverse and reverse milling strong. Uncirculated, and a most desirable specimen. Cost $25.
1850. 1797. Uncirculated cent from the Nicholas' find. Original red and nearly equal to the last.
1851. 1798. A beauty. Beautiful olive of a very light shade, approaching brightness. Uncirculated. Handsome and desirable.
1852. 1803. Small 1-000. Very fine. Olive color.

1853. 1803. Large 1-C00. Very fine. Brown.
1854. 1808. Twelve stars. Very fine. Brown-steel color. Rare so choice. From the famous Merritt sale, $6.
1855. 1809. Very good. Rare. .
1856. 1811. Very good. Rare.
1857. 1813. Fine. Olive-brown color.
1858. 1814. Plain 4. *Extremely fine and sharp.* Brown color. Cost $5.
1859. 1814. Cross 4. As beautiful and choice as the last. Cost $5.
1860. 1816. Uncirculated. Bright red changing to handsome purple.
1861. 1817. Fifteen stars. Exceedingly fine. Choice brown color and very sharp impression, all the stars sharp. One of the best of this variety I have met with. Cost $3.
1862. 1818. Uncirculated. Bright red.
1863. 1820. Uncirculated. Bright red.
1864. 1822. Barely circulated. Every star sharp. An unusually fine impression of fine steel color. Cost $3.
1865. 1831. Very fine. Light olive.
1866. 1832. Very fine, but I think has been cleaned bright. Cost $2.
1867. 1835. Uncirculated. Changing from bright red to a beautiful olive and purple color. Very desirable.
1868. 1836. Uncirculated. Handsome light olive.
1869. 1837. Uncirculated. Brilliant red.
1870. 1855. Slanting 5's. *Proof.*
1871. 1850. Uncirculated. Bright red. 15 pcs.
1872. 1850 to 1856. Very fine to uncir'd. Olive or bright red. 25 pcs.

United States Half Cents, etc.

1873. 1793. Scarcely touched by circulation. Light olive. Rare.
1874. 1794. Very fine. Light olive.
1875. 1795. Thick planchet. Lettered edge. *Very fine.* Strong milling. Light olive.
1876. 1795. Thick planchet, but unlettered edge. No pole to Liberty Cap. Strong milling. Very fine. Light brown.
1877. 1797. Very good. Getting quite rare.
1878. 1800. Very fine. Brown.
1879. 1802. Very good. Rare.
1880. 1806 *Uncirculated. Bright red.*
1881. 1811. Very good. Rare.
1882. 1831. *Light olive proof.* A few very trifling nicks. Sharp impression, and extremely rare.
1883. 1841. Original. *Brilliant bright proof.* Extremely rare.
1884. 1841. Original. Fine. Extremely rare.
1885. 1841. Mint re-strike. *Brilliant bright proof.* Rare.
1886. 1848. Original. *Brilliant bright proof.* Extremely rare.
1887. 1852. Original. *Brilliant bright proof.* Extremely rare.
1888. 1856. *Purple red,* brilliant proof.
1889. **Minor Coinage.** 1856. Flying eagle cent. Uncirculated, mint bloom with proof surface. Rare.
1890. 1864 to 1873. Two cents. Complete set, all brilliant red *proofs* except 1864, 1867, 1868, which are handsome, uncir'd pieces. 10 pcs.

American Colonials.

SILVER.

1891. 1652. Massachusetts Willow Tree Shilling. Crosby No. 2. In good condition for this rare variety, the tree as usual weakly struck, but nearly all distinct; the date and value on reverse weak, but legends nearly all plain. MASAHVSSETS IN—NEWVENG-ENDANDOM. Very rare.

1892. 1652. Oak Tree Shilling. Crosby 2 D. Extremely fine. Rare.
1893. 1652. Pine Tree Shilling. Large planchet. Crosby 1 b. D. Fine.
1894. 1652. Pine Tree Shilling. Large Planchet. 2 a. A 1. Very good.
1895. 1652. Pine Tree Shilling. Crosby 5 B. Large planchet. Exceedingly fine.
1896. 1652. Pine Tree Shilling. Small planchet. Very good.
1897. 1652. Pine Tree Sixpence. Very good.
1898. 1652. Pine Tree Threepence. Very good.
1899. 1783. Chalmers' Annapolis Shilling. Fine.
1900. 1796. Castorland Token. Rev., female tapping maple tree. Silver proof.
1901. 1796. Myddleton Token. "British settlements in Kentucky." Columbia welcomes the infants of Hope. Rev., Britannia seated amid the fallen emblems of Justice and Liberty. Beautiful brilliant silver proof. Very rare.

COPPER.

1902. "New Yorke in America" Token. coined about 1700. Obv., fair; rev., very good. Very rare.
1903. 1723. Rosa Americana Twopence. Very fine and desirable specimen.
1904. 1723. Rosa Americana Penny. Crowned rose. Fine.
1905. 1767. Louisiana Cent. Very good.
1906. 1787. Franklin "Mind your business" Cent. Uncir'd. Brilliant red.
1907. 1785. Vermon Auctori. Rev., "Immune Columbia." Very good. Brown color. Very rare, only about 8 known.
1908. 1785. Same reverse as last, "Immune Columbia," with the "*Ceorcius III. Rex,*" obverse. Obverse very fair and reverse all distinct except the first three and last two letters of legend. Only about fair, but very rare.
1909. 1787. "Liber Natus Libertatem Defendo." Indian with bow and tomahawk. Rev., Arms of New York, "Excelsior." Worn, but with every portion distinct. A very fair specimen of an excessively rare coin. A very fine one brought $105 at the Bushnell sale, the same piece having sold for $90 at the Mickley sale.
1910. 1787. Massachusetts Cent. Horned eagle. Good.
1911. 1787. Massachusetts Cent. Very fine and sharp. Brown color.
1912. 1787. Massachusetts Half Cent. Uncirculated. Light olive.
1913. 1787. Same. Very good.
1914. 1787. "Auctori Plebis." Very good and scarce.
1915. Mark Newby Farthing. St. Patrick and the snakes. Good.
1916. 1788. New Jersey Cent. *Horse head to left.* Good and rare.
1917. 1773. Virginia Half Cent. Uncirculated. Brilliant red.
1918. 1773. Virginia Half Cents. Uncirculated. Brilliant red. *All from different dies.* 8 pcs.
1919. 1773. Virginia Half Cent. One of the handsomest I have seen. Nearly proof. Beautiful glossy light olive, and broad, deep milling. Very desirable. (Cost $3.50.
1920. 1787. Immunis Columbia. Fine specimen of a rare coin.
1921. Kentucky Cent. Thick planchet. Lettered edge. Extremely fine. Light olive.
1922. Kentucky Cent. Thin. Barely touched by circulation. Light olive.
1923. Kentucky Cent. Thin. Fine.
1924. 1789. Motts' Jewellers' token. Fine.
1925. 1794. Talbot, Allum and Lee (New York Cent.) Very fine. Brown.
1926. 1794. Talbot, Allum and Lee. Same as last, but reverse of Birmingham Halfpenny. Uncirculated. Brilliant red. Nearly proof.
1927. 1794. "Franklin press" Cent. Extremely fine. Scarce.
1928. 1795. Talbot, Allum and Lee. Uncirculated. Handsome brilliant red.
1929. 1796. Castorland Token. Bronze proof.

Washington Coins.

1930. 1783. Large head. Rev., "United States." Fine. Brown.
1931. 1783. Same. Small head. Fine. Brown.
1932. 1783. Double head Cent. Very fine. Light olive.
1933. 1791. Cent. Large eagle. Handsome brilliant proof.
1934. 1791. Cent. Same. Fine. Choice brown color.
1935. 1791. Cent. Small eagle. Very fine.
1936. 1793. Liverpool Halfpenny. Very fine. Brown.
1937. Liberty and Security. Large size. Edge lettered : AN ASYLUM FOR THE OPPRESS'D OF ALL NATIONS. *Light olive proof.* Minute scratch above head, bur scarcely marring the piece, which is a gem.
1938. Liberty and Security. Same. Very fine. Light color.
1939. North Wales Token. Very good.

United States Patterns.

1940. 1792. Martha Washington Half Disme. Very good. Rare.
1941. 1822. Half Dollar. Struck impression from the obverse die, in copper. Extremely rare, only two or three known. Very fine.
1942. 1836. Two Cents. Eagle. Nickel proof.
1943. 1836. Dollar. Liberty cap in rays. *Brilliant gold proof.* Rare.
1944. 1837. Feuchtwanger's Three Cents. Arms of New York. Extra fine.
1945. 1838. Half Dollar. Head of Liberty ; reverse, flying eagle. Br. proof.
1946. 1850. Silver Three Cents. Liberty cap in rays. Brilliant proof.
1947. 1850. Ring Cent. Silver alloy. Proof.
1948. 1850. Ring Cent. Same as last, but centre still in. Proof.
1949. 1850. Ring Cent. Same as 1947, but copper proof.
1950. Ring Cent (without date). Copper proof.
1951. 1851. Cent. Liberty seated. Copper proof.
1952. 1852. Ring Dollar. *Gold proof.* Rare.
1953. 1852. Ring Dollar. Gold alloy. Proof.
1954. 1853. Cent. Nickel proof.
1955. 1854. Head of Liberty, without stars. Copper proof.
1956. 1855. Cent. Flying Eagle. Copper proof.
1957. 1855. Cent. Same. Nickel proof.
1958. 1856. Flying Eagle Cent. Similar to regular issue. Copper proof.
1959. 1856. Flying Eagle Cent. Thinner than regular issue. Copper proof.
1960. 1858. Indian Head Cent. Brilliant proof.
1961. 1858. Set of the twelve pattern cents. Four Indian-heads, four small eagles, and four large eagles. Brilliant proofs. 12 pcs.
1962. 1859. Pattern Half Dollars. Head of Liberty ; reverses, "Half Dol.," "½ Dol.," and "50 Cents." Brilliant proofs. 3 pcs.
1963. 1859. Same as last. Rev. "Half Dol." and "½ Dol." Bronze proofs. 2 pcs.
1964. 1859. Half Dollar. Liberty seated. Silver. Uncirculated.
1965. 1859. Cent with reverse of 1860. Proof.
1966. 1861. Five Dollars. Head of Liberty in cap. Copper proof.
1967. 1862. Half Dollar. "God our Trust," on label. Silver proof.
1968. 1863. Half Dollar. Rev., "God our Trust," in field. Silver proof.
1969. 1863. Same. "God our Trust," on label. Silver proof.
1970. 1863. Pattern Three Cents. Obverse same as the old copper cent. Brilliant proof. Rare.
1971. 1863. Two Cents. Same as regular issue. Copper proof.
1972. 1863. Two Cents. Head of Washington. Rev., same as regular issue. Copper proof.
1973. 1863. Cent. Copper proof.
1974. 1864. Cent. Thin planchet, struck in nickel. Uncirculated.

1975. 1866. Three Dollars. Nickel proof. Very rare.
1976. 1866. Silver Dollar. Struck in copper. Proof.
1977. 1866. Two Cents. Nickel. Uncirculated. Rare.
1978. 1866. Cent. Nickel proof.
1979. 1868. Dime. Shield, "Exchanged for U. S. Notes." Rev., wreath enclosing "One Dime, 1868." Silver proof. Very rare.
1980. 1868. One, Three, Five Cents. Liberty head. Nickel proofs. 3 pcs.
1981. 1869. Similar set. Nickel proofs. 3 pcs.
1982. 1869. Set of the beautiful patterns of this year, comprising three each of 50, 25, 10 cents. Splendid silver proofs. 9 pcs.
1983. 1870. Barber's beautiful patterns. Liberty seated with shield, and pole with cap. Dollar, half, quarter, dime, half dime and three cents. Brilliant copper proofs. 6 pcs.
1984. 1870. Longacre's Dollar. Similar to following. Copper proof.
1985. 1871. Longacre's choice design. Indian queen and globe. Dollar, half dollar, quarter, dime, and half dime. Brilliant copper proofs. 5 pcs.
1986. 1873. Set of the six pattern Trade Dollars. Splendid proofs. These proofs are generally hay-marked or dull, but this set is in beautiful, clear condition, and the variety with *plain edges*. This variety is extremely rare, only three or four sets in existence, possibly not that many.
1987. 1878. Barber's beautiful pattern for the Standard Dollar. The rejected design, which was handsomer than the one by Morgan, which was accepted. Brilliant proof. Very rare.
1988. 1879. Metric pattern set. Stella ($4 gold piece), goloid and silver metric dollars. Brilliant proofs. 3 pieces.
1989. Trial impression of the reverse die of the 1836 dollar, struck on a copper planchet. Proof. *Unique.*
1990. Trial impression of the reverse die of the 1856 nickel cent. Struck on a square copper planchet. *Unique.*

Confederate States of America.

1991. Confederate Half Dollar. Silver. Getting rare.
1992. Confederate Half Dollar. White metal proof.
1993. Confederate Cent. 1861. Head of Liberty. Copper proof.
1994. Confederate Great Seal. Electrotype gilt. Mounted under glass in a fine velvet-lined morocco case. Size of seal 56. Beautiful and rare. Also, pamphlet giving history and documents referring to the seal.
1995. View of the Naval Asylum, Portsmouth, Va. *Confederate flag at top.* Rev., "Presented by Council of Portsmouth, Va." Bronze proof. Size 40. Very rare.

U. S. National Medals, etc.

ALL ARE IN BRONZE UNLESS OTHERWISE STATED.

1996. *Army.* Washington before Boston ; Gen'l Morgan ; John Edgar Howard ; Col. Wm. Washington ; Maj. Gen'l Harrison : Maj. Gen'l Taylor. Bronze proofs. Size 28 to 42. Mint medals sold at $1.50 to $2.50 each. 6 pcs.
1997. Maj. Gen'l Taylor. The large medal by Wright for Buena Vista. Rev., battle scene surrounded by two snakes. Beautiful bronze proof in fancy circular wooden case. Size 56.
1998. *Naval.* Capts. Hull, Jacob Jones, Decatur, Bainbridge, Lawrence, Biddle, Stuart, Ed. Prebel. Mint medals. Size 40. Bronze proofs. Sold at $1.50 each. 8 pcs.
1999. *Presidential.* John Adams, Thomas Jefferson, James Madison, James Monroe, John Quincy Adams, Andrew Jackson, Martin Van Buren,

John Tyler. James K. Polk, Zachary Taylor. Rev., clasped hands, pipe and tomahawk. Mint medals. Bronze proofs. Size 40. Sold at $1.50 each. 10 pcs.

2000. James Madison. Indian Peace Medal with the clasped hands, pipe, and tomahawk reverse. *Silver*. Pierced at top. An original presentation medal to some Indian, who evidently wore it. Very fine, desirable, and very rare. Size 43.

2001. Franklin Pierce. Rev., white man pointing Indian to American flag. Size 48.

2002. James Buchanan. Rev., Indian plowing in centre; outside Indian scalping another, squaw's head, bow, quiver, pipe, etc. Size 48. $2.

2003. James Buchanan. Japanese embassy medal. Size 48. Sold at $2.

2004. Gen'l Grant. Inauguration medal. Size 32.

2005. **Miscellaneous.** Capt. Ingraham, for rescue of Martin Koszta. Size 64. Sold at $3.

2006. Maj. Gen'l Scott. For Mexican campaign, from Commonwealth of Virginia. Rev., view of battles. Very large. Size 56. Sold at $3.

2007. Col. Armstrong. Kittanning medal. View of the village in flames. Rev., Arms of Philadelphia. Size 27.

2008. Wreck of steamer Metis, 1872. View of men in boat rescuing people from the water. Size 42. Sold at $1.50.

2009. Henry Clay. Rev., rock bearing a scroll. In velvet-lined morocco case. Size 49.

2010. Chicago fire medal, 1871. View of burning city, angel of destruction above. Rev., Phœnix surrounded by "Made from Chicago Court House Bell." Size 32.

2011. Gen'l Lafayette. Rev., "Defender," etc. Size 30.

2012. Cyrus W. Field. For Atlantic Cable. Size 32.

2013. Mexican War. South Carolina to the Palmetto Regiment. Palmetto tree; rev., men landing from boats, names of battles, etc. Very rare. Size 31.

2014. 1776. Libertas Americana. Very fine. Rare.

2015. 1864. Sanitary Commission Medal. Wounded soldier, etc. Very fine design by Paquet. Size 37.

2016. Set of four Centennial Commission Medals in handsome velvet-lined morocco case.

2017. French Centennial Medal. Helmeted head of Liberty; rev., crossed American flags. Beautiful bronze proof. Size 32.

2018. Egyptian Obelisk medal. Bronze proof. Size 22.

2019. Sage's Historical Tokens. Complete set, Nos. 1 to 14, including the Old Jersey, Old Swamp Church, Carpenter's Hall, etc. Rare as a set. Copper proofs. 14 pcs.

2020. Washington Button. "G. W." surrounded by "Long live the President."

2021. Silver Award Medal of the Mechanics' Institute, San Francisco. A mechanic crowned by a seated female, around whom are strewn fruits, grains, etc., factory, locomotive, etc., in the background. Beautifully designed. Fine proof, size 48, in velvet-lined morocco case.

2022. Silver award medal, California Agricultural Society. Beautiful design. Landscape scene with farm, Cal. big tree, horses, etc.; in foreground, large bear, bust, fruit, etc. Size 28. Weight 1½ oz. Proof.

2023. California Centennial medal, 1876, view of the bay with stage coach, horseman, etc. Rev., train of cars, steamboat, etc. *Silver proof*. Size 26.

2024. "Am I Not a Man and a Brother." Rev., clasped hands. Proof.

2025. "Am I Not a Man and a Brother." Negro in chains. Rev., "Whatsoever ye would," etc. Brass proof. Rare. Size 22.

2026. "Am I Not a Man and a Brother." Small, size 14. Rev., Adam and Eve. Bronze proof. Rare.

2027. Beck's Public Baths. Nude female washing her feet. Rare card.
Very fine.
2028. Hog running; rev., turtle. Brilliant mint lustre. 12 pcs.
2029. 1838. Loco Foco head. Very fine.
2030. Jackson in safe; big-bellied donkey. Fine. Scarce.
2031. Jackson in safe; rev., donkey. *Brass.* Very fine.
2032. Head of Jackson; rev., hog. *Brass.* Extremely fine.

United States Silver.

2033. **Dollars.** 1795. Flowing hair. Very good. Strong impression.
2034. 1796. Large date. *Very* good. Scarce.
2035. 1797. Seven stars facing. Very good.
2036. 1799. Six stars facing. Fine and strong.
2037. 1799. Five stars facing. Good and rare.
2038. 1836. Barely circulated. Surface nearly proof. Rare.
2039. 1841. Nearly or quite uncirculated. Mint bloom.
2040. 1847. Very fine.
2041. 1848. Very fine. Very scarce.
2042. 1853. Extremely fine. Scarce.
2043. 1855. Very fine. But little circulated. Rare.
2044. 1856. Fine and very scarce.
2045. 1873. Brilliant proof.
2046. 1883. Standard. *O. Mint.* Uncirculated. Mint bloom. A proof of
this rare mintage brought $10, July 9th, '84.
2047. **Half Dollars.** 1794. Fair and rare.
2048. 1794. Very much worn. Rare.

The following Half Dollars are catalogued according to Haseltine's Type Table.
An excellent opportunity is given to secure varieties.

2049. 1795. No. 1. Very good.
2050. 1795. No. 2. Very good.
2051. 1795. No. 3. Very good.
2052. 1795. No. 4. Good.
2053. 1795. No. 5. Good.
2054. 1795. No. 6. Good and extremely rare.
2055. 1795. No. 7. Nearly good.
2056. 1795. No. 8. Nearly fine.
2057. 1795. No. 9. Very good.
2058. 1795. No. 10. Very good.
2059. 1795. No. 11. Fair.
2060. 1795. No. 12. Very fair.
2061. 1795. No. 14. Good and very rare.
2062. 1795. No. 16. Fair.
2063. 1795. No. 18. Nearly good. Excessively rare.
2064. 1795. No. 24. Good and rare.
2065. 1795. No. 26. Very good.
2066. 1801. Good but surface sand-worn. Rare.
2067. 1802. Very good. Rare.
2068. 1815. Good and rare.
2069. 1825, '27, '29, '30, '36. Uncir'd, mint lustre or barely touched. 5 pcs.
2070. 1836. Reeded edge. Fine and rare.
2071. 1851. Very fine. Scarce.
2072. 1852. Fine and rare.
2073. 1866. S. Mint. No "In God we trust." Very good.
2074. 1879. Uncirculated. Mint lustre.
2075. **Quarters.** 1796. Worn and plugged over head but date strong.
2076. 1804. Very fair, good for date. Date bold. Rare.
2077. 1828, 1852. Very good. Scarce. 2 pcs.

2078. 1853. *No arrows.* Very good. Rare.
2079. 1860, 1873 (no arrows), 1874. Brilliant proofs. 3 pcs.
2080. 1861. 1879, 1880. Uncirculated. Mint bloom. 3 pcs.
2081. **Dimes.** 1796. Fair. Rare.
2082. 1798. Very fair. Rare.
2083. 1801, 1805. Worn. Good dates. 2 pcs.
2084. 1805, 1807. Good. 2 pcs.
2085. 1811 and same over '09. Very fair and very good. 2 pcs.
2086. 1814. Large date. fine; Small date, good. 2 pcs.
2087. 1823, 1828, 1835, 1838, 1853 (no arrows), 1860 (stars). Good. 6 pcs.
2088. 1869, 1879, 1880. Uncirculated or proof. 3 pcs.
2089. **Half Dimes.** 1794. Very fine impression, date sharp, but large hole above head plugged. Rare.
2090. 1795. Very good. Scarce.
2091. 1795, 1800. Worn. Good dates. First pierced. 2 pcs.
2092. 1797. Fifteen stars. Very good. Scarce.
2093. 1800. Very good. Scarce.
2094. 1801. Good, but a few nicks. Rare.
2095. 1803. Somewhat battered but rare. Very fair.
2096. 1838 (no stars), 1844. Fair and good. Scarce. 2 pcs.
2097. 1838 (stars), '40, '47, '53, '62, '68, '71, '73. Uncirculated. 8 pcs.
2098. **Silver 3 Cents.** 1851 (P. and O. Mint), '52, '58 to '62. Uncir'd. 9 pcs.
2099. 1855. Very fine. Scarce.
2100. 1873. Brilliant proof. Rare.

United States Cents.

2101. 1793. Wreath. Fair and rare.
2102. 1793. Chain. Slightly better than last. Rare.
2103. 1793. Chain. Very fair impression but date tooled.
The following 1794 cents are catalogued according to Dr. Maris' work.
2104. 1794. No. 3. Sans Milling. Very good.
2105. 1794. No. 5. Young Head. Good.
2106. 1794. No. 7. Crooked 7. Very fair.
2107. 1794. No. 9. Crooked 7. Good.
2108. 1794. No. 12. Scarred head. Fair.
2109. 1794. No. 16. Separated date. Good.
2110. 1794. No. 17. The Ornate. Very good. Bold.
2111. 1794. No. 20. Fallen 4. Good, better than usual.
2112. 1794. No. 21. Short Bust. Very good.
2113. 1794. No. 32. Shielded Hair. Very good.
2114. 1794. No. 34. The Plicæ. Fair.
2115. 1794. No. 36. The Plicæ. Good.
2116. 1794. No. 37. The Plicæ. Good.
2117. 1794. No. 38. Roman Plicæ. Good.
2118. 1794. No. 40. Many haired. Very good.
2119. 1794. No. 47. Very fair.
2120. 1794. Unclassified. Poor and fair. 5 pcs.
2121. 1795. Lettered edge. Good and scarce.
2122. 1795. Thin. Very good.
2123. 1796. Liberty Cap, good. Fillet Head, fair. 2 pcs.
2124. 1797. Indented edge. Fine. Brown color. Strong milling.
2125. 1797. Curious variety, with an F showing under M in "America" on reverse, a die cutter's error. Bold impression, the hair scarcely touched. Light brown. Rare.
2126. 1798. Nearly fine. Bold.
2127. 1801. Very good.
2128. 1802. Die cracked over ATE on rev. Fine. Light color.

2129. 1803. Large 1-100. Fine.
2130. 1803. Small 1-100. Fine.
2131. 1804. Fair for date. Rare.
2132. 1806, 1808, 1810, 1812, 1813. Good lot. 5 pcs.
2133. 1806, 1808, 1809, 1812, 1813. About fair to good. 5 pcs.
2134. 1809. Good and rare.
2135. 1811. Good. 2 pcs.
2136. 1814. Cross 4, fine. Plain 4, good. 2 pcs.
2137. 1816. Very fine. Bold impression.
2138. 1817. Extra fine. Beautiful light olive.
2139. 1817. Fifteen stars. Fine and unusually bold. Handsome brown.
2140. 1819. Small date. Uncirculated, bright changing to olive.
2141. 1820. Uncirculated. Olive.
2142. 1816, 1818, 1820, 1821, 1823. Good to very fine. 5 pcs
2143. 1822. Fine. Light olive.
2144. 1824. Very good. Brown.
2145. 1825. Fine. Light brown.
2146. 1826. Fine. Light brown.
2147. 1827. Barely circulated. Bold impression. Light olive.
2148. 1828. Large date. Very good. Strong.
2149. 1830. Remarkable break in die under date. Good. Rare.
2150. 1832. Fine. Large lettering on reverse.
2151. 1835. Head of '36. Small date. Strong milling. Fine. Brown
2152. 1836. Broken die. Small stars. Very fine. Light brown.
2153. 1837. Plain hair-string. Small lettering. Fine. Light color.
2154. 1839. Head of '40. Very good. Brown.
2155. 1839 over '36. Good and rare.
2156. 1840. Large date. Fine. Light brown.
2157. 1840. Small date. Fine.
2158. 1842. Large date. Uncirculated. Light olive.
2159. 1838, 1842, 1844. Good and very good. 3 pcs.
2160. 1845, 1846 (Dutch 6), 1847, 1848, 1849. Fine lot. 5 pcs.
2161. 1850 to 1854. Uncir'd lot. Partly bright. 5 pcs.
2162. 1857. Large and small dates. Barely cir'd. Partly bright. 2 pcs.

United States Half Cents, etc.

2163. 1793. Fine. Rare.
2164. 1794. Very good.
2165. 1795. Thick. Unlettered edge. Good.
2166. 1797. Fair. 1800. Good. Scarce. 2 pcs.
2167. 1802. Good and rare.
2168. 1811. Good. Rare.
2169. 1837. Half Cent worth of pure copper. Fine.
2170. 1852. Very skillful alteration.
2171. 1803 to 1857 inclu. 1810. Early dates very good. later dates very fine.
      No duplicates. 24 pcs.
2172. 1864, 1865, 1868 Two Cents. Mint lustre. 3 pcs.
2173. 1864 to 1884. Bronze cents. Uncirculated. No duplicates. 8 pcs.
2174. 1858. Pattern cents, four Indian heads, two small and two large
      eagles. Proofs. All different. 8 pcs.
2175. 1836. First steam coinage at U. S. Mint. Bronze proof.
2176. Franklin Cents. Connecticut, etc. Poor Colonials. 19 pcs.
2177. Am I not a Woman and Sister? and store cards. Good. 13 pcs.
2178. Priced sale catalogues, includes Anthon, Part II. etc. No duplicates.
      18 pcs.

New Jersey Cents.

The following are catalogued according to Dr. Maris' work.

2179. 1786. 15 L. Very good.
2180. 1786. 16 L. Fair.
2181. 1786. 18 M. Bridle variety. Good. Scarce.
2182. 1786. 23 R. Good.
2183. 1787. 43 d. Very fair.
2184. 1787. 46 e. Good.
2185. 1787. 48 g. Very fair.
2186. 1787. 63 s. Very good.
2187. 1788. 67 v. Fair.
2188. 1787. 32 T. 38 Y. 39 a. 51 i. 64 t. Poor to fair. 5 pcs.
2189. **Connecticut Cents.** All labeled according to Crosby. Includes FNDE. horned bust and other scarce pieces. Poor to very good. No duplicates. 19 pcs.

Hard Times Tokens.

The following are catalogued according to Haseltine's list.

2190. No. 1, 2. American Institute. Very good. 2 pcs.
2191. No. 3. Card of W. A. Handy. Very good. Rare.
2192. No. 6, 8. Lafayette. Walsh and Richard's cards. Good. 2 pcs.
2193. No. 9. Same as 8 but New York in full. Good. Rare.
2194. No. 10. Jackson with money purse. Fine. Olive.
2195. No. 11. Hog running. "Down with the Bank." Fine.
2196. No. 15. Jackson in money-chest. Uncirculated. Olive.
2197. No. 17, 18, 19. Varieties of last and one with ship on rev., fine. 3 pcs.
2198. No. 21. "Speed the plough." Walsh's card. Very fine.
2199. No. 24. Bucklin's Book-keeping. *Head to left.* Poor but very rare.
2200. No. 25, 26, 27. Turtle and donkey. Varieties. Very fine. 3 pcs.
2201. No. 29, 30, 31, 34, 35. Very fine lot of the ship tokens. No. 30 and 34 are scarce, former pierced. 6 pcs.
2202. No. 38, 39, 40, 41. Varieties of the Phoenix tokens. Fine lot. 4 pcs.
2203. No. 44, 46, 47, 48, 49, 50, 51, 53, 54, 60, 62, 63, 66. Varieties of the 1837 heads, including also the Crossman, Jarvis, Deveau cards. Fine lot. 13 pcs.
2204. No. 58. Large handsome laureated head. Very good. Very rare.
2205. No. 68, 69. Eagle, 1837. Crossman and Maycock cards, fine. 2 pcs.
2206. No. 85. Am I not a Woman and Sister? Very choice.
2207. No. 86, 87, 88. 1841 head, varieties, very good. 3 pcs.
2208. No. 89, 90, 92. Merchants' Exchange. Fine. 3 pcs.
2209. No. 84, 94, 99, 100, 101, 102, 106, 111. Loco Foco, Riker, Duseaman. Anderson, March, Sise & Co., Smith's Clocks, Bucklin's Book-keeping. Very good. 2 pierced. 8 pcs.

U. S. Silver, Copper, etc.

2210. 1869. U. S. Brilliant proof set. Complete. Scarce. 10 pcs.
2211. 1826, 1827, 1828, 1830, 1834. U. S. half dollars, uncir'd. Mint lustre. 5 pcs.
2212. Stonewall Jackson medal (size 32) in case. Two medalets. Uncir'd. 3 pcs.
2213. 1796 Frankfort dollar. Uncirculated. Mint lustre.
2214. 1738 Dollar of the Dutch East India Co. Uncir'd. Rare.
2215. Japan. Itzebue. Oblong. Uncirculated.
2516. Honduras, Costa Rica, Nicaragua, New Grenada, Uruguay, Chili (25 cent size). Peru, Uruguay (dime size). Foreign silver. Fine lot. 8 pcs.
2217. Nicaragua, Peru, 1879, provisional (5). Nickels. V. fine. 6 pcs.

2218. Roman denarii. Marc Anthony, Galba, Trajan, etc. V. fair lot. 5 pes.
2219. Roman family denarii. Rubria, etc. Includes a rare one with double Janus head. Also, small Greek silver of Augustus and drachm of Dyrrachium. Fair to good. 11 pes.
2220. Urbs Roma (wolf and twins). Small bronze. Very fine. Old charm, copy of shekel, etc. 5 pes.
2221. Foreign coppers (25 uncir'd.) Japan, Sardinia, Ceylon, etc. 48 pes.

U. S. Cents.

The following cents I think are all different, though I have not time to carefully compare. Among the later dates will be found some quite desirable specimens.

2222. 1793. Wreath. Lettered edge. Very fair.
2223. 1793. Wreath. Lettered edge. Fair.
2224. 1793. Liberty cap. Very fair.
2225. 1794. Fallen 4, separated date and others. Fair to v. good. 6 pes.
2226. 1795. Thick and thin. Both very good. 2 pes.
2227. 1796. Liberty cap (2 var's). Fillet head. Fair to v. good. 3 pes.
2228. 1797 (3); 1798 (3) varieties. Fair to very good. 6 pes.
2229. 1799. "Liberty" weak, head good, date *very good;* rev., very fair. Rare.
2230. 1799. An alteration, but pretty well done ; 1809 copy. 2 pes.
2231. 1800 over '99, 1801, 1-000, etc. Other varieties of both dates fair to very good. 7 pes.
2232. 1802, 1803. Marked varieties. Four quite fine. 13 pes.
2233. 1804. Very good. Rare.
2234. 1805, 1806, 1807, 1807 over '06, 1808. Varieties. Fair to nearly fine. 10 pes.
2235. 1809. Good and rare.
2236. 1809. Nearly equal to last.
2237. 1810, 1810 over '09, 1811, 1811 over '10. Good and v. good. 4 pes.
2238. 1812, 1813, 1814. Fair to very fine, one of 1812 partly bright. 6 pes.
2239. 1816, 1817, 1818. Uncirculated. Olive and br. red. 3 pes.
2240. 1817. Fifteen stars. 1819 over '18. Both fine. Brown color. 2 pes.
2341. 1816 to 1825. Many varieties, including 1821 (2), 1823 and 1823 over '22, 1824 (2), etc. Good to fine. A desirable lot. 28 pes.
2242. 1827 to 1830. Nearly all quite bold. Several fine and of light color. Varieties including large and small 1828, cracked dies, etc. of 1830. 13 pes.
2243. 1826, 1831, 1833. Very fine, choice light olive. 3 pes.
2244. 1831 to 1836. Varieties. Good to fine. Desirable lot. 17 pes.
2245. 1834, 1835 (large 18). Very fine. Choice light brown. 2 pes.
2246. 1837, 1838. Varieties. Plain and beaded hairstring of '37. Choice lot. 7 pes.
2247. 1839. Silly head. Very fine. Light brown.
2248. 1839 to 1845. Good to very fine. I think all different. 15 pes.
2249. 1845 to 1849. Very fine lot. Olive or brown. One partly bright. 11 pes.
2250. 1850 to 1857. Handsome lot, including some sharp light olive pieces. 18 pes.
2251. 1838, 1849 to 1856. Bright red lot. Desirable. 11 pes.
2252. 1856. Flying eagle nickel cent. Extremely fine. Rare.
2253. 1858 to 1882. Nickel and bronze cents. All different. Uncir'd. Mint lustre. 23 pes.
2254. **Cents.** 1793 to 1857. Also Franklin "Mind your business" cent. The 1793 is a Chain, fair for date. 1799 miserably poor, but may be genuine. 1804 poor, but genuine and guaranteed. 1809 good. 1811 fair. Most of the early dates including 1794, fallen 4. 1797, 1805,

1806, are good or very good, the later years good to uncirculated.
Many fine and bold. A desirable set. 68 pcs.

2255. **Half Cents.** A collection embracing 26 different dates including 1794,
1797, 1800, 1810. 1811, fair to good. Also other dates good to uncir'd,
with varieties. To fill spaces, copies of 1793, 1795. 1796, 1802, 1811,
1831. 1836, 1840 to 1849 sm. date. 1852. A desirable set. 50 pcs.

2256. **Stamps.** 1870. 1, 2, 3, 6, 7. 15, 90 cts. Unused. 7 pcs.

2257. Postage due. 1, 3, 10 cts. Uncancelled. 3 pcs.

2258. Newspaper. 1865. 5, 10, 25 cts. Unused. 3 pcs.

2259. Newspaper. 2. 4, 6, 8, 9, 10, 12 cts. Unused. 7 pcs.

The following are unused, marked SPECIMEN.

2260. Agriculture. 1 to 30 cts. Complete set. 9 pcs.

2261. Executive. 1 to 10 cts. Complete set. 5 pcs.

2262. Justice. 1 to 90 cts. Complete set. 10 pcs.

2263. Post Office. 1 to 90 cts. Complete set. 10 pcs.

2264. State. 1 to 30 cts. Complete set. 10 pcs.

2265. War. 1 to 90 cts. Complete set. 11 pcs.

2266. Treasury. 2, 3, 6. 7, 12, 15. Uncancelled. 6 pcs.

2267. Interior. 3, 6, 12. Barely touched in cancelling. 3 pcs.

2268. 50 cent note. Fessenden, red back. Autographic signatures of *Allison*
and Spinner. *Very slightly* circulated. Very rare.

www.ingramcontent.com/pod-product-compliance
Lightning Source LLC
Chambersburg PA
CBHW022159020726
47496CB00008B/2796